Second Chances

A billionaire Christian romance for adults...

A complete Christian romance for adults, suitable for over 18s only due to sex scenes after marriage.

International model Donna thought she had it all, until she was in a car crash that killed her beloved fiancé.

She was devastated, but then she found out that he was sleeping with other women while they were together.

Returning home with little to no trust for men, she decides to end her modeling career, devote her life to the Lord and help in the community as needed.

It's through this community work that Donna meets billionaire Marcus, a handsome former basketball star who is immediately taken with her.

Neither can deny that sparks fly, but will Donna be able to get over her distrust of men and let Marcus in?

Or is she doomed to relive her past for a second time?

Find out in this heart felt, passionate Christian romance by bestselling author Shannon Gardener of African American Club.

Suitable for over 18s only due to sex scenes between a hunky billionaire and his Christian beauty.

Get Free Romance eBooks!

Hi there. As a special thank you for buying this book, for a limited time I want to send you some great ebooks completely **free of charge** directly to your email! You can get it by going to this page:

www.saucyromancebooks.com/physical

You can see a the cover of these books on the next page:

These ebooks are so exclusive you can't even buy them. When you download them I'll also send you updates when new books like this are available.

Again, that link is:

www.saucyromancebooks.com/physical

Contents

Chapter 1

"I cannot tell you how much help you have been to us during the last two months Donna. You have been such a treasure." Janet Dawkins told her gratefully. She ran a 'Comfort Touch' agency that offers help to people who needed it especially to those confined to a wheelchair and since Donna had become a 'member', people have been requesting her more and more. Janet secretly thought that maybe it was because of the way she looked.

Tall with a slender willowy body with gently curving hips; the former international model was so striking that people usually turned around to take a second look. She had beautiful coffee and cream complexion with dark hair cropped close to a small straight face and large dark expressive eyes. Her lips often curved to reveal beautiful white teeth with a small gap in the middle.

"Thank you Janet." Donna said with a wave of her hand. It was her redemption and even though she could not undo the life she had lived before, she was going to spend the rest of her life trying to be the person God wanted her to be. She had been given another chance and she was grabbing it with both hands!

She hummed a tune as she made her way to her small powder blue compact car. It was the middle of summer and she had learned to appreciate each day. She sat there and took in the petunias wilting a little in the fierce sunshine but their beauty apparent nonetheless and she noticed that someone had turned on a sprinkler to give the thirsty plants some moisture.

She switched on her engine and drove off slowly. It had taken her almost a year after the accident to get behind the wheel but she had done so little by little gaining confidence again.

It was a little after five and she made her way home, adjusting the thermostat in her vehicle as she felt the humidity kicking in. It had been forecasted that they would be having thunderstorms and she could see the clouds getting heavier by the minute.

She pulled up at the gate and got out, walking up the little pathway and inhaling the heavy scent of roses, lilacs and hydrangeas as she made her way up to the front door.

"Honey is that you?" her mother called out from the kitchen.

"Yes mom and I could smell you apple pie from out in the street." She said with a smile as she hurried into the kitchen. The house was a small three bedroom, two baths building which her mother had made into a cheerful abode with brightly colored throw mats and curtains. She made the best pies in the neighborhood and was always in demand.

"How was your day?" Lydia Brown asked her daughter, holding her soft cheek up for the usual kiss.

"Very good," Donna said enthusiastically accepting the slice of pie and the glass of milk her mother had put out for her. She had gotten her looks from her mother and her height from her father who had died four years ago from a heart disease. They had grown up their only child in the church until she had decided that she needed more and had left to try her hand at modeling. "I told Mr. Benjamin what you told me earlier about having a lot more faith in a larger than mountain God and to look for the positive in every situation."

"How did he take it?" Lydia asked in amusement. She knew Frank Benjamin to be a crotchety old man with misery stamped on his well lined face and did not take too kindly to people telling him that his life could be so much worse. He had been in a farming accident that had robbed him of both legs and he railed at fate every single day.

"He told me to get out of his house." Donna said with a smile, using her fork to scrape the special sauce her mother used on the pie and licked the fork appreciatively. "I told him I would be back tomorrow for our usual session."

Lydia stared at her daughter reflectively for a little bit as she put the pies on the cooling rack on the counter. She had an order for a dozen apple pies, two dozen Lemon meringues and a dozen blueberries and she was halfway through her baking. "I am so proud of you." She told her softly, hugging the beautiful girl to her. She did not like to remember that almost two years ago she had almost lost her only daughter and she constantly thanked the Lord for bringing her back in one piece and the miracle He had wrought in her life.

"Thanks Mom." Donna told her hugging her back. "Now what do you want help with?"

*****

Later in her room, she sank on her bed wearily. She had taken a quick shower and pulled on an old cotton nightgown that she had come back home and saw in her drawer. The room had been the same, only a fresh coat of pale peach paint had made a difference. The bed was the same: white painted wood with canopy over it and she had not bothered to remove it.

She had been so careless and proud. An international model jet setting all over the world and a handsome man beside her who had given her an ostentatious diamond to show the world that she was taken. It was only when he had died in that car crash that had almost taken her life, she had discovered she had not been the only woman in his life, that there had been others; baby mamas as well.

They had been driving home from a party at two o'clock in the morning drunk on alcohol and stupidity when his red sports car had slammed into an embankment. The road had been slippery because it had rained earlier, there was no traction for the tires to grab and the brakes had not held. She had woken up in the hospital three days later with her mother at her bedside and learned that Kevin had died on the way to the hospital. It had been such a wasteful and foolish life and one that she knew she had not enjoyed as she thought she would. It had taken another three days for her mother to get her to talk to her and when she learned that her modeling days were over due to a small slightly discernible scar on her forehead she had cried for two days before deciding to pack up her stuff and go back home with her mother.

She had given her life to the Lord after her mother had gently showed her that she had been given a second chance to make things right with her life. She had given away most of her fancy wardrobe and had given the ugly expensive ring to Kevin's mother without looking back. She had saved up a lot of money and it was there sitting in her account; she was not sure she knew what to do with it yet because her mother had told her she had everything she needed and she did not need her money. "I am sure you'll find use for it eventually dear."

Tears shimmered in her dark brown eyes when she remembered the infrequent phone calls home and the quick visit back home when her father had died to attend the funeral and without spending one night at home she had flew back because she had a shoot in Malibu the following day.

Her mother never mentioned how badly she had treated them and for that she was grateful but it always came back with painful clarity. She had sent money every month, writing generous checks like a dutiful daughter but that had been easy to do because she had the money; she never had the time though.

With a trembling sigh and a prayer she pulled the sheet over her.

*****

Marcus Wellington looked at the latest sportswear critically. It was a new design that he wanted to test out on the market but he was not sure it was ready. It was supposed to contour itself to the wearer's body as they moved and be light enough make it seemed as if you were not wearing any clothing. He had been a pro basketball player until he had knocked out his knee in a game that had ended his career for good three years ago. Instead of sitting down and moaning about it he had got up, dusted himself off and opened a sporting goods store and within a year he had branched out all over the country; to now owning a billion dollar company that was a household name.

Wellington Sports sponsored a lot of local sports because he had decided that he needed to give back and support other athletes as well. He had come all this way with only a mother to bring him up as his father had disappeared as soon as she was pregnant.

He put aside the clothing and picked up the framed picture of his gentle yet strong mother who had made sure he grew up knowing right from wrong. He had decided to visit her this weekend to see for himself how she was faring. He had bought her a magnificent home the first time he had earned a large sum of money, although she had protested she only needed a small home, and had made her retire from doing housework for people. She had broken her hip a few weeks ago and was confined to a wheelchair but she had told him that he had hired so many helpers that she barely had the chance to brush her own teeth.

He replaced the photo with a smile. There was nothing he would not do for her.

There was a discreet knock on the door. "Come in." he called out.

His secretary Linda walked in. They had almost gotten involved when she came to work for him a year ago but he had pulled back. As beautiful and chic as she was he was not into getting involved with his employees; fortunately they had gone on to be more than employer and employee but friends as well and she was now engaged to be married.

"We have the sports magazine on the line that has been wanting to do an interview and to find out whether or not the new sportswear is ready and you have a one o'clock with your favorite charity." She told him with a smile.

"Thanks Linda," he said with a returning smile. "I take it they are already at the basketball court?"

"Ready and waiting and all suited up." She said with a nod.

He had taken on a team of under twelve boys and had invested time and money in them as he tried to make a difference in their lives.

"I'll be right there." He told her as he took the call.

*****

Marla Wellington welcomed her cheerfully, a wide smile on her chocolate brown face. Donna had been assigned to her for several weeks as a companion and she had learned the woman loved to read, especially the Bible. "My dear you look much better than those pictures in the magazines."

Donna had gone past the periods where her past life and mention of her career brought her to tears and had learned to accept the various comments in stride. "Thank you, you're too kind. I brought you an apple pie my mother baked." She said with an answering smile of her own.

The house was a show piece and was sure it suited the attractive but simple woman. She knew it had been bought by her famous son and appreciated the gesture but there was too much space for one person. His picture was prominently displayed over the mantelpiece and she took in the wide white smile and the smooth chocolate brown skin and the low cut black waves. He was very handsome and she suspected that he knew it very well. She looked away. Men like Marcus Wellington did not interest her in the least bit.

She turned her attention the pleasant woman who told her thanks for the pie and she should put it on the kitchen counter.

She had met two women on her way in and had seen one of them dusting the furniture and the other one watering the plants out front. She hoped that what he was doing was not for show. Who was she to judge? She had done the very same thing.

They chatted about sports and fashion briefly and they had a lively discussion about the Bible.

"Men, my dear, have been deserting their roles since the beginning of time." Marla said with a tinge of amusement. They were out beside the pool sipping lemonade and eating slices of her mother's delicious pie. The pool looked inviting and cool but the palm trees planted in rows made way for a pleasant breeze that cooled their warm skin. "Take Abraham for instance; instead of telling his wife Sarah that he was not going to sleep with another woman because he was going to wait for the promise God made him, he succumbed to her urgings and in the end they made trouble for all concerned."

"But in all that I have learned, it's to see the awesome goodness of God," Donna commented, gazing across the well manicured lawn. It was really a beautiful place and a peaceful one at that. "I have recognized it in my life as well."

Marla looked at the girl shrewdly. She had read about the crash that had taken the life of her fiancé and had ruined her promising career and was surprised to hear that she was back home and doing what she was doing. "Do you question the curve that life has thrown you?"

Donna clasped her hands in her lap. She was wearing a floral summer dress that showed off the smooth light brown curves of her elegant shoulders and her long neck. She had no make-up on except for a little lip gloss but her beauty shone like the mid day sun. "I did at first." She said with a small smile that curved her full bottom lip. "I cried for two days and threw a pity party the likes you had never seen! Then my mom with her gentle logic, told me that I was alive and that was another chance. I had been given the gift of life and I should grab it with both hands. I did not believe it at first but eventually I got there."

"God has a way of making us see things our way," Marla said contemplatively. "I am happy you were able to see the good in this situation my dear, a lot of people don't."

"So am I." she murmured.

*****

Page 17

"Hey Mom what's going on?" Marcus held the phone between his shoulder blades and kicked off his sneakers. He had been playing a strenuous game of basket ball with the youngsters and he was feeling all of his twenty-seven years. He had been getting ready to stand underneath the shower and let it beat against his skin when the phone rang.

"I hope you won't change your mind about coming by this weekend," her soft calm voice came over the phone.

"Would I let down my favorite mother?" he teased.

"Your only mother," he was reminded. "I met such a delightful young woman today."

Marcus stifled a sigh. His mother spent her days trying to set him up with a 'good woman' from his hometown. He had tried to tell her that he needed no help in that area but his mother did not take kindly to what she referred to as the 'fast women' he was involved with. "Mom, I am sure she is very nice and I am also sure she would not appreciate being singled out for your son."

"I did not say anything about being singled out honey. I just think it is time you settled down and start a family. You are not getting any younger and the Lord does not approve of the lifestyle you are living."

"Mom did you call me just to preach or to tell me how proud of me you are?" Marcus deflected her train of conversation effectively as he always did.

"I am proud of you son, you know that." She told him softly.

He hung up after promising her that he would eat something before going to bed. "Maybe some soup," she suggested.

He rolled his eyes as he hung up the phone. His mother always treated him like a twelve year old and was the only woman he allowed to tell him what to do.

He went into the ultra modern black and silver bathroom and stepped into the shower stall and adjusted the temperature to allow the water to sluice down his chocolate brown skin. He pressed his hands against the glass walls and thought about the night he had spent with Kaila.

She was a sleek sports model he had met a few months ago when they had been looking for someone to model the sportswear for women. She was Caucasian with jet black hair and green eyes and red pouty lips, his mother would definitely not approved, he thought wryly. Ah but the things they did in bed was something that had him going hard even now. She had called him and wanted to come over but he had told her he was tired and the truth was he did not usually invite women to his 'bachelor pad' as he referred to it as because he did not want them to think that something was there when it was not.

He always went to their apartment and made up for not taking them to his place by buying them expensive jewelry.

He stepped out of the shower and reached for the towel, drying himself and went into the kitchen completely naked. He caught a glimpse of himself in the full length mirror and noticed with satisfaction his muscled body. He kept in shape by still playing hoops and working out in his well equipped gym both at the office and his apartment. He was satisfied with the result. He was not ready to settle down yet, he was having too much fun being single.

*****

Marla Wellington hoisted herself on the bed. She refused to have anyone help her get ready for bed because she valued the alone time in her bedroom. She was almost sixty years old and in spite of the hard life she had had during the times when she had to scrub peoples' floors and bathrooms when she was pregnant with her son. She still managed to look younger than her age.

She picked up her Bible and started reading but found her mind drifting to the beautiful young woman she had spoken to today. She had always admired her pictures in the magazines but found that the girl looked even more beautiful in person. Suffering had added character to her appearance as it always did. She had read about her fiancé and had seen pictures of them in the papers and had thought the man looked like he thought too much of himself.

As soon as Donna had left, a thought had germinated in her mind and she had been mulling on it for the whole evening. With a smile curving her lips she prayed. God can make the impossible possible.

*****

"Mom, this is nice," Donna murmured. Her mother had made cold cuts and cucumber sandwiches and tall glasses of lemonade. They were sitting out on the front porch enjoying the afternoon sun. It was the second week of August and thankfully a slight breeze had sprung up to cool the evening.

"I think so dear." Lydia leaned back against the porch swing and looked across the yard slowly. The edges needed trimming she would have to get Lincoln from church to come and give her a hand. Her husband used to do it but he was gone, bless his soul and she still missed him.

"How was your visit?" she asked her daughter. The girl's profile was turned away from her as she stared out on the garden. Such a beautiful woman, she thought fondly.

Donna told her about her conversation with Marla and the opulence of the house. "She is such a down to earth person Mom and really upbeat about her situation."

"As we all should be," Lydia commented sipping her cold drink. "So many times we forget to count our blessings and that's what's wrong with us today. A lack of thanks."

Chapter 2

She was invited to an end of summer barbecue at Marla's house. She had spent a wonderful week with her and had become friends. Donna found herself looking forward to going there each morning.

"Are you sure you are up for it?" she had asked the woman in concern.

"You sound just like Marcus," Marla grumbled good-naturedly. "I am far from being an old doddering person with the last breath to draw you know."

"Of course I know that," Donna had told her with a smile. "In that case, I will be happy to come and Mom will be bringing her pies as a contribution as well."

"The Lord blesses her!"

Donna dressed with special care. For the first time since she had been back, she pulled out her suitcases she had brought back with her. Not that they had the power to set her backwards into the past but she had decided she was through with that life. Besides this was a small town and everyone led a simple life.

She rummaged through the pile of clothes and pulled out a sarong type dress with a myriad of colors with fringes at the end and held it up to look at it. It was perfect and it was also cool. The weather had been brutal for the past few days and the dress would suit the occasion. She looked through her jewelry box and found the perfect earrings: big gold hoops and matching bracelets. She was going to wear her strappy tan and gold sandals with it.

She went for a little make-up, dusting foundation on her coffee and cream skin and adding nude color eye shadow and lip gloss. Lydia stood in the doorway and watched her daughter expertly apply her make-up and was reminded that she had had a different life not so long ago, a more sophisticated life. She constantly thanked the Lord that it had not been the death of her. "It always amazes me that one so beautiful could come from your father and me." She said softly.

Donna looked up and met her mother's eyes in the mirror. "I got whatever looks I have from you Mom. I spent years making a living from the looks God gave me and never using it for his glory, now I don't put much stock into it. True beauty comes from having a relationship with God."

"Beautifully said darling," Lydia came into the room and stood behind her, placing her hands on her shoulders. "But don't be ashamed of how God made you."

"Thanks Mom," Donna said gratefully, placing her hands over her mother's briefly. "Ready?"

Lydia nodded. She had on a lovely floral dress and a large orange hat to shield her face from the sun. "I put the pies inside the car and a large igloo of my special iced tea."

"I am sure she will appreciate that."

*****

The place was alive with people and music. Donna recognized some of them from church. Marla waved them over to where she was with a tall handsome man standing beside her chair. Donna recognized him instantly from the photos in the house and from his pictures in the sports section of the papers.

"I would like you both to meet my son." She said beaming with pride.

"How nice to meet you!" Lydia exclaimed reaching out a hand for him to take.

"And this is Donna, the angel who has been assigned to me since last week." Marla continued.

Ever since she had entered his line of vision, his breath had caught. His mother was right, she was not only beautiful, because he was used to beautiful women, but she was extraordinarily beautiful!

"I hope I may call you Donna," he said quietly, reaching out a hand to grasp, his chocolate brown skin looking dark against her coffee and cream complexion.

"You may," she told him with a slight smile, quickly pulling away her hand and turning towards Marla. "You didn't tell me you were inviting the whole neighborhood," she teased as she clasped the woman's hand gently.

"I was afraid you would not turn up if I had." Marla told her with a smile. "Marcus would you show Donna around and let her eat something while Lydia and I talk a little bit? I want to see if I can convince her to tell me her secret recipes."

Donna was about to protest that she wanted to stay with them but Marcus was already taking her arm and leading her away.

"I am sure you have better things to do than to babysit me," she told him coolly as they made their way to the table laden with a variety of food.

"Actually, no," he told her mildly. He could feel her resistance to him and wondered if it was just him or if she had no tolerance for men in general. He had read what had happened to her in the papers and he could not imagine what she had gone through. "What would you like to eat?" he asked her taking up a paper plate.

"I am perfectly capable of fixing my own plate," she proceeded to take up a plate and started to place food on it.

"I see you are a fan of potato salad," he said teasingly. "It's fortunate that you don't look like you put on weight, as a matter of fact-"

"I know your mother told you to show me around and all that," she told him quietly, pouring herself a glass of lemonade. "But I know my way around and I will be okay."

He was being politely dismissed and he knew it. He wanted to tell her he did not need to be dismissed by her. He just had to make a phone call and he would have women running to be with him. He felt the anger rising up inside him and he tamped it down. She was nothing to him anyway.

"You are right," he told her coldly. "I have better things to do anyway."

He walked away with long strides and Donna could see his tall frame above the other people as he made his way towards some children playing with a ball. She sighed and took the plate half filled with food and her drink and went over to where some church people she recognized were seated.

"Hey Donna!" a guy named Michael called out to her.

"Hi Michael, how are you?" she greeted him cordially. He had saved a seat on the bench for her. She had known him from the time she was living here and at that time he had been on the church choir, he was now an assistant pastor at the church.

"I am doing well. It's great to see you and you always look beautiful." He commented. She recognized Mabel, a girl she had been to school with and Jessica, Michael's wife.

"Thank you." Donna said briefly with a smile. She had been to church since she had been back but had not taken part in any of the activities, even though her mother had said she should, she did not feel comfortable doing so yet.

"We were thinking of forming a young people's forum at church where we have different activities. We have asked Marcus for his help in forming a sports team and we were wondering if you would form a group with the young women where you could teach them deportment and how to conduct themselves." Jessica said to her with a smile. The woman looked like the epitome of calmness and peace and had an air of tranquility around her that gave her an ethereal glow.

"I will let you know." Donna told her.

"Good enough." The woman said graciously. They chatted about the community and the outreach program they were planning on implementing and sat there watching the children frolicking in the pool.

*****

Marcus watched as she laughed at something the guy beside her said and the way the smile lit up her exquisite face. He had walked away from her but after a few minutes he had wanted to go back and force her to talk to him. He was talking with the young men present but his mind was not with them one bit. He loved the way the dress hug her curves and her page boy haircut highlighted her large dark eyes. He found himself looking at her more than once and he realized he was interested.

He had been asked to set up a sports area at the church and he had told them yes, that meant he would be spending more time here. He had felt like such an idiot when she cut him off so abruptly and he was not used to feeling like a fool. His mother had told him gently one day after the team had won a game and he had been named the 'MVP'. "Don't let it go to your head son. Glory only belongs to our Lord. I am not saying you should not feel good about the benefits of your hard work but never let it have you believing that you are better than anyone else."

He downed the icy glass of delicious iced tea and with a determined stride went over to where she was still sitting with the rest of people. He had not built a billion dollar company by giving up.

"Marcus we were just talking about you!" Jessica said in delight. He saw her stiffened at the mention of his name. Good, at least she was not indifferent to him. "I was just telling Donna about the young people group and what we planned to do. Both of you have been the face of success for many years and the young people could stand to learn a thing or two about your secret and how to maintain a positive attitude."

"So we will be working together?" he asked her, a smile on his handsome face.

"As I told Jessica, I will think about it. I am not sure I have anything to share. Success is relative and it depends on how you look at it." Donna said coolly. "If you'll excuse me, I have to go and check up on Marla." With that she left.

Marcus followed her with his eyes. She had done it again and he was damned if he was going to follow behind her like a fool. To hell with her! Who did she think she was? He had tried reaching out to her two times now and she had shunned him so that was it for him. He was done.

*****

Donna fought back tears as she raced inside to the bathroom. She had never had such a strong reaction to a man before and she did not know what was going on. She was always polite and she had asked the Lord to mend her of her haughty ways. She had been doing so well until Marcus Wellington. She had been rude to him twice and there was no excuse for that. She had been doing so well. She had made up her mind after finding out that she had not been the only one in her fiancé's life and although a lot of people did not know she had been holding out for marriage before she gave herself completely to him.

"I love you Donna and I respect your wishes to wait." He had told her and she had loved him for his patience, never dreaming his tolerance of her desire to wait had been due to the fact that he was getting it from several others. She had just been an ornament for his arm when they were seen together. She washed her face and reapplied her make-up, making sure there was no trace of tears on her face before going back out to join the others.

"Marcus has decided to come to church with me tomorrow," Marla was saying in a pleased tone. She and Lydia were still in conversation and several other women their age had come by to join them.

"How wonderful!" Lydia said waving to her daughter. "I love when they acknowledge that they need a little religion in their lives."

Donna went to sit underneath the shade of a palm tree and rested back against the lounge chair, closing her eyes briefly. The heat was making her wilt a little bit and although it was a little after five and there was a slight breeze blowing, her skin still felt clammy and sweaty.

"You look like you could use a dip in the pool." Her eyes flew open and she saw him standing there looking down at her. His body was blocking the sun from her and she sat up abruptly with the intention of telling him she wanted to be alone.

"Please don't leave," he said quietly, taking a seat on a nearby stool. "I don't know what I did wrong but I apologize for whatever it is. I hope we can start over. Hi my name is Marcus Wellington and I am pleased to meet you." He had his hand out and Donna knew it would be past rude not to take it.

"Donna Brown." She told him briefly, taking his hand and letting go instantly.

"My mom talks about you all the time," he told her, pretending not to notice how quickly she had pulled her hand away, at least she was not hightailing it away from him. "She calls you her angel on earth."

"I enjoy being with her," she admitted to him with a brief smile. "She is quite a woman."

"I thank God everyday for a mother like her. She raisedme without a father and did a fine job of it." He told her. He wanted to keep her there, talking to him. He had told himself that he was going to stay away from her but he had noticed she had gone away by herself and being the glutton for punishment that he was, he had decided to try again.

She looked at him for a moment and then nodded.

"What do you think about the program they are planning on implementing?" he asked her, feeling out desperately for a topic that would keep her talking to him. He was attracted to her and he had never felt an attraction so deeply before.

"I think it will work if the commitment is there," she told him quietly. "Are you planning on committing yourself to the cause Marcus?" He loved how she called his name.

"Are you?" he countered.

He saw a glimmer of a smile appeared on her full lips and he felt himself tighten in desire. She had lips made for kissing. He dragged his eyes away from her lips and look into her lovely dark brown eyes.

"Good question." She nodded her head. "I will give it careful thought and let them know."

He knew the subject was exhausted and he searched desperately through his mind to find something else to talk about. "I understand you gave your life to the Lord." He said for want of something better to say.

"Was there a question?" she asked him in amusement.

She had a way of making him feel like an idiot, he thought grimly. "I was on the choir at church when I was a teenager. I am afraid I have departed a little bit from the faith."

"Only a little bit?" she asked him raising one tapered brow.

He laughed, his deep laugh attracting quite a few stares. "Okay you got me. I have departed a lot from the faith."

"We all do that at one time or another," she looked away from him, her gaze caught by a couple feeding each other with a single hot dog and looked swiftly away. Marcus caught the moment and he remembered she had lost the man she loved in that terrible car accident some years ago. He wanted to ask her about it, ask if she still loved him and was still grieving but he did not dare, that would be too intrusive. "Ever think of finding your way back?"

He almost sighed in relief at her question. He had thought she would have ended the conversation then and there. "I will one day," he said honestly.

"Hopefully it will not be too late." She murmured looking at him for a moment and Marcus knew she was referring to the time she had been in the accident.

"I am sorry," he said softly, holding her gaze with his.

She nodded, looked away and did not say anything else. He sat there not wanting to leave but knowing that she had finished talking and wanted to be left alone. "I want to work on this thing with you, will you consider it?" he asked her hesitantly.

"Why?" she asked him baldly.

"Because I think we would make a good team." He told her with a grin, showing beautiful white teeth in a dark face.

"I will think about it." She told him briefly. He stood up just then and as he was about to leave he turned back to her and said: "I want to see more of you." And without waiting for her response he walked away leaving her staring after him.

*****

They left at seven with Donna giving Marla a gentle kiss on the cheek, telling her that she threw the best barbecue and she had enjoyed herself immensely.

"I will be looking for you in church tomorrow," she told the girl fondly.

Marcus was at the grill and Donna made sure she avoided that area; what he had said to her had disturbed her and she did not want to think about it.

"You are quiet," Lydia glanced at her daughter curiously. She had seen her talking with Marcus Wellington and wondered what that was about. She knew she had been hurt terribly in the past, not that she had told her everything but she had told her some things and her heart grieved for her.

"I am just a little bit tired from the heat," Donna forced a smile to her lips. She had turned up the air conditioning but the humidity was still very much a factor.

"Quite a handsome young man that Marcus," she murmured casually.

"I suppose he is," Donna kept her eyes on the road.

"And quite talented as well. I understand he busted his knee and was unable to play again but he did not allow that to stop him, he went on to turn his handicap into something positive. You have to admire that."

"Is there a point to all that Mom?" Donna asked her a little impatiently, wishing she would get off the subject of Marcus.

"He is quite a young man dear and he reminds me of you." Lydia told her gently, settling back against the seat and looking out the window.

*****

Donna cleaned off her make-up methodically as she had been taught to do when she was in the modeling business. She had a special expensive cream she used on her face and although she did not use make-up much these days; when she did she made sure to use the cream. Why had he said that to her? Did he think that because of what had happened to her that she was an easy target?

She went to take a shower and get rid of the sweat and dust from her skin and then climbed on the bed, her Bible opened before her. She found herself thinking how he had looked. He had worn khaki shorts and a green T-shirt that showed off his muscled forearms to advantage. He was tall, even to her five feet ten; she had just come up to his shoulder. With a deliberate movement, she shook him from her thoughts and went back to her Bible.

*****

Marcus sat there in the bedroom he always used whenever he came to visit his mother. He had seen Donna leaving and he had watched her walking away. He had wanted to go and say something to her but he had refrained from doing so. His mother had not stopped singing her praises and asking him what he thought of her. He could not very well tell his mother that he was attracted to her. He was going to church tomorrow and he hoped he saw her.

He got up and stood in front of the full length mirror. He had taken a shower and retired for the night, making sure his mother was comfortable in bed. She was tired but happy so he had not bothered to scold her about overdoing it.

"I am so happy you are here honey." She had said with a gentle smile.

"So am I Mom." He had told her.

Chapter 3

The day had turned out to be pretty mild for the ending of August. The heat of the day before had lessened considerably. Donna had worn a simple pale green sleeveless dress and gold accessories.

"You look lovely dear," Lydia commented as they got ready to leave.

"Thanks Mom," she said. "You don't look too bad yourself." She added with a smile.

There was quite a turn out for the service and the sermon was based on David and Bathsheba and the consequences of our actions.

Donna looked around and her eyes were caught by Marcus. He was sitting beside his mother in the row opposite hers and his eyes caught hers before she could look away. He smiled at her and she nodded, quickly looking away. She sat back and enjoyed the rest of the sermon not once glancing in his direction.

She was roped into serving snacks to the Sunday school department and was in the middle of doing so when he came into the auditorium. He was dressed in black dress pants, white shirt and a sports jacket. He looked handsome and relaxed and very sure of himself.

"I wondered where you had gone off to," he teased as he came over to the table. She gave the little girl a plate and smiled at her murmur of thanks. Her mother was somewhere around talking to some of the sisters.

"Hi Marcus," she greeted him coolly. His cologne was the same one she had smelled yesterday, something tangy and expensive and it suited him.

"Wonderful sermon." He grabbed a plate and started helping her with the sharing. She noticed the stare he was receiving from the number of women scattered all around. He probably knew they were looking at him.

"Do you believe we suffer the consequences whether good or bad of whatever we do?" he handed the plate to the little girl with pig tails and a smile.

"If the Bible say it then it must be true." She said coolly as she shared another plate. She was becoming too aware of him and she did not like it one bit.

"I was taught to read the Bible at a very tender age. I used to think of it as a necessary evil but my mother made the stories comes alive. I used to think that David had wandering eyes even though he tried to control it."

"Marcus," she turned to face him. "I don't know what you are doing but I need to tell you right now," she looked him square in the face and could not help but noticed how clean shaven and strong his jaw was. "I am not interested in having any sort of relationship. I am exploring the one I am in with the Lord and that's the only one I am interested in right now. So please stop coming up to me and striking up a conversation to try and test the waters. I am not interested."

He held her gaze a while longer and then continued sharing. She stared at him in frustration, hiding behind a smile as two little girls came over for their plates. He waited until they were gone before he responded. "I know you have been hurt and I know that you don't trust men. All I am asking for is friendship right now and whatever comes after then I will work with it. I am interested but I understand that these things take time." He looked at her as he said it and Donna did not answer him. She did not know what to say to him just then.

She started to walk away but his soft deep voice stopped her. "You make me feel something I have never felt before and I would like to get a chance to explore it."

She did not turn around but continued walking and she could feel his eyes burning holes into her back.

She made the rounds and said goodbye to Marla and several others and chatted with Jessica a little bit, promising her that she would let her know by tomorrow what her answer would be.

*****

"Mom, how did you meet dad?" Donna asked her mother.

They were sitting on the front porch eating the salad and fried chicken they had prepared as soon as they had arrived from church. Donna had changed and put on shorts and a T-shirt and her mother was wearing a plain white house dress. It was almost four o'clock but the place was still bright and sunny and the heat was not very evident.

"I met him when I was taking a pastry making class at the community center. He was teaching English Literature to the underprivileged youths." Lydia told her.

"Did he approach you?" Donna asked reaching for a corn on the cob and listening with interest.

"He did," Lydia nodded. "I was there for a week when he approached me and asked me my name." She smiled at the memory. "I looked him over for a minute and then told him that I do not give out my name to strangers."

"What did he say?"

"He persisted until I finally told him my name and we started going out together." Lydia said with a smile. "I fell in love with him the second week and we got married two weeks after."

Donna stared at her in amazement. "Mom are you serious?"

"As a heart attack." Her mother said with a laugh. "It was a whirlwind romance and we did not see the sense of waiting when we were sure of each other. Donald agreed of course and we were married in a small ceremony right in the community center."

"Ever regretted it for one minute?" Donna asked lightly.

"Not even for one second." Her mother told her firmly. "Were you in love with him?" she asked her gently. She did not say his name but they both knew who she talking about.

"I thought I did," Donna gazed off into the garden and watched as a squirrel ran up a tree. "I was caught up in all the hype and the glossiness of the business. He was so handsome and charming and he told me all the right things. I was living in the moment and I guess that meant I bought into the shallowness of it all. When I learned he had died, I did not know whether to feel relief or grief and when I discovered what he really was I definitely felt relief. Is that awful?"

"A little bit," Lydia reached out a hand and touched her reassuringly. "You were being human and we tend to think of ourselves first. What you had with him was not the real thing honey and I hope going through that terrible experience does not cut you off from opening your heart to the real thing."

"How will I know it's the real thing? And how do I trust myself to know if it's real?" Donna asked spreading her arms.

"You have put your trust in God so let him guide you and he will point you in the right direction."

*****

Later that night Donna found herself unable to sleep. She had been doing so well with her life, picking up the broken pieces and making a fresh start and now Marcus was making her aware again. She definitely was not ready for that sort of thing, especially with someone like him.

*****

He was there when she went the next morning and the surprise at seeing him there stopped her in her tracks. He was not dressed for the office and she thought he would have been gone back to his office or wherever it was he went.

"Mom came down with a little flu," he said greeting her at the door. "I guess the excitement was too much for her."

"Oh I am so sorry!" Donna exclaimed, wondering if she should have called first. "Should I just say hi and leave?"

"She would never forgive me if I let you leave." He told her with a grin. "She's already giving me grief for missing work to look in on her."

"So you are leaving?" she asked him innocently heading towards the room.

"You don't have to sound so relieved," he said dryly. "I will be leaving a little bit later today and I wanted to discuss something with you."

"What?" she asked stopping and turning to look at him. She had worn a short floral skirt that flared around her long legs when she stopped and a sleeveless cotton blouse that outlined her small breasts. She looked cool and beautiful in spite of the heat.

"So suspicious." He teased. "I spoke to the physiotherapist and she said that mom should be exercising more. What do you think?"

"It's up to her," Donna said with a shrug. "She is still in touch with all of her faculties so I think she should make her own decisions."

She turned to walk away and he captured her arm. "You keep running away from me, why?"

"I am not running away, I am walking away. You are reading too much into it." Donna told him, ignoring the shiver of awareness that went through her at his touch. "Now if you'll excuse me I need to go and check up on your mother."

He did not let her go. "Have dinner with me this weekend," he said urgently, he had drawn closer to her and she smelled his elusive cologne.

"I don't want to," she told him bluntly, pulling away from him and this time he let her go. "You're wasting your time Marcus." She told him as she walked away.

"It's my time to waste," he called after her. "And I don't think so."

She recovered enough to be cheerful and pleasant around Marla, reading to her and chatting about this and that. Even getting into a heated debate about some sports game, but all the time she was praying that when she left the room she would not run into Marcus. He had rattled her and she did not want to admit it but his touch had sent off something inside her that she did not want to admit.

She left the room when the nurse came and sat by the pool. He was nowhere around and she gave a sigh of relief.

God, she breathed. She did not need this complication in her life right now, please take it away and let me concentrate on my relationship with you, please. She had closed her eyes and when she opened them he was standing right in front of her.

"I am hounding you I know," he told her his deep voice quiet. "I went and told my mother I was leaving because I did not want to make you feel uncomfortable but I have to tell you this before I leave. I am attracted to you," he stopped when he saw her recoil and with a sigh he crouched down beside her. "I am not asking you to go to bed with me, I am asking you to have dinner with me." He took her hand and raised it to his lips, opening it and resting his lips on her palm. She felt the desire shivered through her and she started to pull away. "NO," he said softly. "Look at me Donna," he pleaded. "I know what you have been through and I respect that. I know what you probably think of me and I also respect that but I am telling you I cannot stay away from you. I have just met you and I cannot stop thinking about you."

She dragged her hand away from him and stood up forcing him to do so. "I am not interested!" She was trembling from desire and rage. "I am not going to be your next conquest and if you continue, I am going to be forced to tell your mother I won't be coming around anymore."

They stood there in front of each other and then with a groan he dragged her into his arms. Donna resisted at first and then when his mouth touched hers it was like an explosion had been set off inside her. She opened her mouth underneath his and she spread her hands against his muscular chest, feeling the play of his muscles underneath her fingers.

He brought her up against him, his hands kneading the small of her back. His mouth moved over hers hungrily and he felt his control slipping.

Donna surfaced enough to realize what she was doing; her desire spiraling out of control. She dragged her mouth from his, her breathing ragged, her body shaking from the aftermath of the raging emotion. She had been kissed many times before in the past but she had never felt like this, not even close.

"Stay away from me," she told him shakily. He stood there looking at her, his chest heaving, his hands clenched.

"I can't," he muttered and without another word he spun on his heels and left, striding away from her.

Donna stood there trying to get her emotions under control. He was right; she did not want him to stay away from her either. Was that making her a hypocrite? She had never been with a man before apart from kissing and she had only been mildly aroused but this felt like a bush fire raging out of control. She was surprised she had been able to push him away.

*****

She stayed outside long enough to make sure that he had gone. She saw when his BMW drove away and only then did she go back inside the house. By that time, she had composed herself sufficiently enough to be able to function properly.

Marla was feeling sufficiently better so Donna wheeled her out to the garden, near the pool. It did not help one bit due to the fact that she spoke about Marcus the whole time.

"I did not have to tell him that we were poor and could not afford certain things," she said with a fond smile. "He understood he had to go without a lot of things and promised me that one day he was going to be able to put me up in fine style. He is a good son Donna," she said looking at the girl sitting beside her quietly, the Bible in her lap. She had seen the way Marcus looked at her over the weekend and she had smiled with the knowledge that her son had finally met a woman who did not fall down in adulation in front of him, he was going to have to work hard to gain this one's trust.

"Just allow the Lord to do the healing." She told Donna quietly.

*****

Marcus bounced the ball off the court and sent it into the hoop forcefully, holding on to the hoop before falling gracefully to the floor.

"Hey man what's up with you?" It was Tyler, his friend and the CFO of the company. It was late afternoon at the office and they usually came down to the court along with a group of others, either to work out in the gym or get in a ball or two. Marcus had been down on the court for the past hour and a half and his dark chocolate skin glistened with sweat.

"Working off some steam," he muttered throwing the ball to his friend who caught it deftly. They had been friends for years through high school and college. Tyler came from a well to do family and had gone to an Ivy League college, whereas Marcus had gotten by on a sports scholarship. In spite of the differences in their backgrounds, they had remained fast friends. Tyler was a child of God and was happily married with two children.

"What's up?" he dribbled the ball and then passed it to his friend.

"I met this girl," Marcus began as he dunked the ball inside the hoop.

"Ah!" Tyler said with a grin. "The mighty Marcus has been touched by the great emotion."

"What?" he looked at his friend startled. "No, no it's just that I am attracted to her and I have never felt an attraction so strong before."

"As I said, floored by the great emotion," Tyler grinned.

"Shut up man," Marcus said mildly, throwing the ball to his friend forcefully.

"So who is this wonder woman?" Tyler passed him a bottle of Gatorade from the mini fridge there and took one for himself.

"She was a super model at one point and was in a terrible car accident that claimed the life of her fiancé and put her in the hospital for a couple of weeks." Marcus sat on the floor and guzzled the liquid thirstily.

"Donna Brown," Tyler said, understanding dawning and his eyes widened. "She lost her career and her fiancé in one go. That's rough man." He sat beside his friend and looked at him curiously. "You have women climbing over each other to be with you and you're looking at Mount Everest?"

"The body wants what the body wants." He shrugged. "She has done nothing but rejected me."

"What do you expect man? The girl has been through hell and back. She is not going to be open to anything remotely resembling a relationship right now. And besides I read that the fiancé was a womanizing bastard who had several baby mamas in the ring."

"I know man." Marcus said with a sigh. "I dug up some old newspaper articles on the whole thing and I realize that her distrust in men is well placed. I kept looking at her pictures in the papers and realize that if it is at all possible she is even more beautiful now."

"You have your work cut out for you." Tyler slapped him on the back. "But knowing you, you are not going to stop until you climb that mountain. God speed my brother." He grinned, getting up in one fluid movement. "Now how about a round before I go home to my beautiful wife and kids?"

*****

Donna drove to the 'hill'. In the past when she had something bothering her she would walk several blocks from her house and go out to a slight slope she had discovered when she was a child.

Being an only child she had found ways of entertaining herself and had pretended that the 'hill' was a little castle and there were princesses living there. One of the princesses happened to be her best friend and she had named her Arielia.

Even in teenage years she had still gone there when she had been troubled or when her mother told her she was not reading her Bible enough. She would go there to meditate and talk to her 'friend'.

She parked the car at the foot of the hill and walked the rest of the way. She had taken a towel from the car and spread it out on the grass. She laid there looking up at the clear blue sky. The temperature had dropped somewhat as September arrived and there was a cooling breeze going through the trees.

She had discovered her beauty when she was in high school as little by little she had grown from a lanky shapeless girl into a startlingly beautiful woman with gentle curves. She had been accepted into the popular crowd and had ousted blond hair, blue eyed Gabrielle from the most popular position; a title she had never wanted. She had been sought after by boys and girls alike and had been told countless times that she had the body and face of a model. She had not paid it any mind because her parents had raised her in the church and had not put much stock in outward appearances. She had been drawn to the idea of it when she had been showed magazines depicting women in beautiful outfits and exotic locations and the idea had started to grow in her mind.

She had gotten the chance of a lifetime when she had sent her head shots to several agents in town and had gotten a call almost immediately.

She looked across at a bird making a nest in the nearby tree and several beautiful butterflies flitting from one plant to the next. God's beautiful creatures, doing what they were made to do. With a weary sigh she closed her eyes, Marcus came unbidden to her thoughts. He had put his mouth on hers and she had found herself melting into him. With embarrassing clarity, she remembered how his mouth felt on hers and how his body molded itself to hers and how right it had felt.

Chapter 4

Her two weeks with Marla was up much to their disappointment but she promised she would keep in touch. She would visit and they would always see each other at church. Marcus had not been by and she found herself missing him and aching for him. She deliberately took her mind off him and concentrated on the new assignment she had been given.

Ninety three year old John Franklin was a joy to be with. He had been through two wars and had seen so many things that he was an absolute font of information. He also knew the Bible from cover to cover and ended up teaching her many things. He had outlived his wife and two children and had only grandchildren and great grandchildren to contend with. He still lived at home, the home where his parents had lived and where he had lived with his wife and children. He had made the additions of two bedrooms and a bathroom and a front porch with his own two hands as he put it and was not leaving there until God said it was time to go home. He was full of answers and good advice and Donna loved talking to him.

"What's a beautiful young lady like you doing with an old man like me?" he asked her teasingly.

It was their second day together and they were on the porch playing cards. The weather had mellowed and the temperature had cooled somewhat allowing them to be out on the porch with the breeze blowing through the trees and cooling their skin.

"There is no place I would rather be," she told him with a smile. There was a service that came and prepared his food for him but he usually managed to get snacks for himself. She had brought an apple pie her mother had made for him.

"Not good enough girly," he had said firmly, placing his winning cards on the table with a wide smile. "Why aren't you wearing some man's gorgeous diamond ring on your finger?"

"Because I am not ready yet." She told him, shuffling the cards together. She did not feel the slightest bit offended by his questions and found herself answering them truthfully. "I made a mistake some time ago and chose the wrong person and am now making sure that I do not make that mistake again."

He nodded sagely and looked at her with his bleary dark brown eyes. His skin was leathery and wrinkled but he still managed to walk upright when he did. "It's okay to be cautious girl but it's not okay to cut yourself off from love because some man did you wrong. There are still some good men out there, so be careful that you don't let your past color your present."

"I'll try not to," Donna said softly. "Now let's play cards and you are not going to cheat me again."

"I don't know the meaning of that word." He told her with a wicked grin.

*****

"You have a visitor," her mother gave her a curious look as she made her way out to the front gate just as Donna was pulling up. She had seen the Porsche parked a little way away from the gate and had wondered curiously who was visiting her mother.

"Who?" she asked, her heart thudding because she already knew the answer.

"You will see. I am going to get some supplies from the supermarket. I am running short on baking products and I have an order from church." With a wave she got into her car and drove away.

He came out onto the porch as soon as she stepped up and she stopped short, her eyes noticing the dark gray dress pants and the burgundy shirt. He had removed his tie and opened the top two buttons of his shirt. He looked vital and terribly handsome. "What are you doing here Marcus?" she asked him striving for calm.

"I wanted to talk to you but I have a feeling that calling you would not make any sense because you would probably hang up on me and then I realized I did not have your number." He shoved his hands into his pockets and looked across at the yard rioting with flowers. "I can't get you out of my mind," he told her bluntly and Donna's throat hitched as he came nearer to her. "I keep thinking about you and this has never happened to me before and I don't know what to do about it."

He made his move finally reaching out to lift her chin. She was on the bottom step and he on the top and he was looking down at her. "Can you tell me what to do?"

His voice had dropped a decibel and Donna felt it again, the fire raging inside her at his nearness and she wanted to sink into him.

His hands framed her face, her exquisite face that he had not been able to get out of his head, even when he was sleeping, he was dreaming of her. "Stop me," he breathed against her lips.

But she couldn't, not even if she was forced to do so, she could not stop him even if she had wanted to. He took her lips with his, tongue probing hers, his body tightening as he felt her sag against his.

Donna felt as if she was floundering in a pool of water that was closing over her head and any minute the current was going to take her in; that is if she did not surface; she had to surface, she had to try. She dragged her lips from his and stepped back out of his arms, her chest heaving uncontrollably. She had to take several deep breaths before she could speak.

"Please leave," her voice wanted to be firm but it came out weak and fluttery and she hated it.

"No," he told her quietly.

She stared at him confounded, not sure she had heard him right.

"I am not leaving until I talk to you." He repeated coming down the steps. Donna backed away from him. "We need to talk." He took her by the hand and she went with him to the porch swing. "I know what you went through-"

"The hell you do!" She jumped up using anger as her defense. It was the only one she had and she was going to use it. How dared he think he knew what she went through! "How could you? Do you know what it felt like to wake up in a hospital bed, to find out that the man you were going to spend your life with had been playing you all long? Do you know the humiliation I went through? The gripping disbelief and the bitter pain of not only losing him but also losing the respect I had for him and thinking that everything he ever said to me had been a lie? Do you know what that feels like?" she was breathing hard, her hands clenched at her sides.

She had never felt such a rush of anger as she felt now and she had thought she had had everything under control. She felt the shame and confusion wash over her as soon as she had finished. This was not happening! She was a child of God! She did not portray anger like this anymore and besides she was done with the past, wasn't she?

Marcus sat there staring at her fury. God she was magnificent. He heard everything she said and his heart went out to her. He wanted to smash the guy's face in, feeling sorry that he was already dead.

"I am sorry," she hugged her arms around her and he felt her pain as sure as it had happened to him.

"For what?" he asked her quietly. He stood up and she shook her head but he came forward and took her into his arms. "For telling me how you feel?" He closed his arms around her and she found herself resting her head against his chest. She was wearing sandals and he seemed to tower over her. "I am not going anywhere Donna, so I am asking you to accept that. Anything you want, I am here and if it takes me the rest of my life, I am going to prove to you that I am not him and I would never hurt you, unless I was not aware I was doing so. I promise you that."

She burst into tears. He lifted her as easily as he was lifting a basketball and sat with her on the porch swing letting her cry inside his arms, getting his expensive shirt wet but he held her to him and rocked her gently.

She felt as if she had been crying for an entire day and when she was finished she still sat there curled into his arms, feeling the security and peace she had not found in a long time. Eventually she lifted her head and felt the acute embarrassment wash over her. She started to get up and he held her.

"Not now," he told her huskily. "I don't want to let you go, please let me hold you for a little bit." She relented and he pulled her back against him. She was aware that her mother would be back any minute now and see them like this.

He did not say anything and neither did she; clinging to him was what she needed right now and she was holding on to it. It was several minutes before she pulled away and got out of his arms and he did not stop her.

"How about dinner?" he asked her lightly. He looked at her standing there before him and even with her eyes slightly swollen from crying so much; she was still the most beautiful woman he had ever seen. However long it took, he was going to stay and show her that he was not setting out to hurt her.

"I know a little place that we could go to and eat as much crab as you want," he smiled at her gently.

"Crab?" she looked at him confused, glad that he had not mentioned her crying jag.

"You like crab don't you?"

"I have not eaten crab in a long time," she said with a glimmer of a smile.

"There you go!" he told her with a wide smile. "I'll sit here on this porch swing and wait until you go and get ready."

She hesitated a little bit and then went to the bathroom. She stood under the shower and let it beat down on her, the warm water soothing her battered emotions. She was going to dinner and she was not having any regrets. She had cried in his arms and he had held her to him like a broken doll. She had thought she was all cried out but she was wrong.

She selected her clothes carefully. The evening had cooled down and there was a slight breeze so she put on black pants with a high waist and a sleeveless purple blouse that went well with her coffee and cream complexion. She put make-up on and tiny gold knobs and bracelets. She wore black shoes with small heels. Her mother still was not back so she called her and told her that she was going out to dinner with Marcus.

"Good for you baby," Lydia said in a pleased voice. "I'll see you later."

"I am ready," she said as she stepped out on the porch. He stood up slowly and looked at her. Why did it give him such a punch in the gut to find out how beautiful she was?

"You take my breath away every time," he told her ruefully, reaching up a hand to capture the curve of her cheek.

"Marcus," she began, her dark brown eyes holding his.

"I know," he dropped his hand and took her hand in his, holding on firmly as they walked to his car. She was used to luxurious vehicles and was not really impressed by the butter soft leather as she slid into the passenger side. She had been in plenty in her glamorous career and she found she did not think much of it anymore.

He had put on his jacket and she realized that he looked very confident, like the successful business man he was. He took her to a little remote 'shack' that looked like a cabin. It was called the 'crab place' and the manager was a friend of his.

"Marcus my brother!" the middle aged African American with bulging muscles called out, slapping him on the back. Inside it was cool and elegant with padded chairs and music playing softly. There were not many people there and the man, Angel as he was called because of the tattoo of an angel on his forearm led them to a corner booth. "How is my favorite sports star?"

"Here to eat some of your best crab. I told Donna you were the best in the business so I want you to prove me right." Marcus told him with a smile.

"For such a beautiful woman? Absolutely, no problem." Angel said walking away his muscles bulging.

"We used to race together some time ago," Marcus told her. He reached across the small table to take her hands; he could not seem to stop touching her. "I used to be wild and out of control because I let my celebrity status get to my head until my mother sat me down and set me straight. From then on, I tried to keep my head on my body and the same size it is now." He smiled a little bit. He picked up one of her slender hands and stared at it; at the delicate veins and the short but beautifully cut nails with no artifice on her fingers. "I want you Donna," he looked up at her. "I have never felt this way before and right now maybe I am bungling it but I have to say it."

She was saved from answering just then as Angel himself came forward with a steaming platter of flavorful crab and another bowl of white rice. "I have asked them to bring a big jug of iced water," he grinned, revealing very white teeth against a dark face. "You are going to need it."

Donna tasted the crab tentatively at first and then she dug into the curried crab and rice. As spicy as it was, she enjoyed it immensely. They talked. He told her about his life as a basketball player.

"I enjoyed it because I love the game and I got on well with my team mates." He told her quietly, leaning back against the padded seat.

"Do you miss it?" she asked him, drinking down the water thirstily to parch her stinging throat.

"At first yes, but as the years went by I found that basketball wasn't everything and it did not make any sense to live in the past. I have excellent memories of the games and the experience but I enjoy what I do now." He looked at her. "How about you?" he asked her. "Do you miss gracing those magazines with your beauty?"

She looked down at her hands clasped on the table, her long lashes shielding her eyes. "Sometimes." She commented. "I miss going to places I have never been before and the rush to get clothes on and make-up and the dizzying excitement." She admitted. "But I am not pining for it. I never thought I would settle down to a quiet life where God is in the center of it all. But I am and I would never go back to that lifestyle."

"And you don't see it as giving up?" he leaned forward and forced her to look at him.

She looked at him startled that he had asked her that. "I gave up that life for something more tangible." She told him truthfully. "I thought I was happy but I never was. I was caught up in all the excitement and I let it carry me along with it."

"Success tends to do that to us sometimes." He said.

They had finished eating and were enjoying the music playing softly in the background. "I want to see you again." He said suddenly. "I want to take you out to dinner and the movies and maybe to a ball game or two and eventually I want to make love to you."

Her breath stopped and she found she had to make a concerted effort to breathe. "Marcus you need to stop-"

"I can't," he took her hands. "I don't know where this is going and I respect that you are not going to fall into bed with me but I want to see you again and again and I will not be taking no for an answer."

He leaned forward and before she could pull back he took her lips with his. Donna opened her lips underneath his and sank into the kiss, not caring or unable to care whether they were been watched. He explored her lips hungrily, his penis uncoiling like a sleeping snake and stiffening inside his underwear. He wanted her so badly that he felt the desire beating inside him like so many drums. This time it was he who broke off the kiss. He dragged his mouth from hers and holding her hands tightly with his, he settled back against the seat. "We need this," he told her huskily.

He took her home shortly after and he held her hand even when she tried to pull it away. The night air cooled their skin as he had let the top down. The wind tousled her short hair against her face.

"Cold?" he asked her solicitously, taking his eyes briefly off the road and looking at her.

"No," she told him with a smile.

He parked the car at the gate and turned to her.

"Don't touch me right now please Marcus," she pleaded with him. "I have listened to everything you've said and I know you are right but I need to be alone for a while to think about this. I have been hurt pretty badly and I need to think about that for a little bit and then wonder if this is something I want to do. I cannot think when you touch me," she laughed shakily staring past him outside at the lights that decked the street sides. She was scared. Frightened of the feelings he evoked inside her and the way she responded to his slightest touch. She had never felt this way before and it scared her.

"I can't not touch you," he told her softly, his hand reaching out to trail a finger against her lip. The cranberry colored lipstick she had been wearing had disappeared and her natural lip color was seen. "I cannot help it and I know I am supposed to respect your wishes but, not touching you?" he left the question unanswered as he pulled her closer to him.

With a soft cry she surrendered. He rushed her lips, moving over her mouth with a hunger and desperation that took her breath away. She clung to him and gave back with all she had in her. He took it and gave her something that he had never given another woman before except the woman who gave him life; his heart. He felt his heart beating dramatically inside his chest and he groaned against her mouth as he tore his lips away from hers and rested his forehead against hers.

"I want to say so much to you right now but I am not going to because I know you are not ready yet and I am going to wait, just don't ask me to wait too long." He fixed her hair gently and kissed her cheek softly before moving away from her. "Goodnight Donna." He told her softly and she pulled the door open in a daze and stepped out of the car.

He waited until she had gone inside before he drove off, stopping a little way down the street to regain his composure and to see if he could will his erection to go down but that was asking the impossible. He leaned back against the head rest and breathed deeply. He was in love with a woman he barely knew. A woman he had met a few short days ago. What the hell was wrong with him?

With a twist of the steering wheel he turned the car around and headed to his mother's place.

Chapter 5

He took her out almost every evening. She protested she did not have the time but she went just the same because he said he wanted to get to know her and she should get to know him as well.

He took her to the movies, it was a comedy that had them laughing together until he started to kiss her. He came to church with her and they started the project together, it was going pretty well. He was getting pretty frustrated about not being with her all the way and sometimes he had to stay away from her in order to control himself.

He had taken her to a basketball game on the weekend and she had enjoyed herself immensely. He found himself watching her as she ate a hot dog and rooted for the team. She had worn a faded pair of denim pants and a beautiful cashmere sweater that hugged her curves lovingly.

He had plied her with snacks and she had asked him laughingly if he wanted to get her fat. She had stopped laughing as her gaze was captured by his and she saw the look in his eyes. "Marcus," she had breathed, making matters worse.

He had not kissed her, reining in his passion with a superhuman effort but after that he had not been able to enjoy the game. This thing with her was getting to him and he was getting angry and short with whomever he was around. His mother had told him to be patient the night he had dropped her off and gone around there.

"I am not sure I can," he had told her ruefully, pacing the length of her bedroom.

"Marcus Orlando Wellington," she had said sternly. He knew when she called him by his full name that he was in trouble. "Don't you dare try to ruin this. Donna is a classy lady and deserves your patience. Besides it is a sin to have sex before marriage so please keep your libido in check."

He had stared at the woman who had given birth to him as she lay there propped up against her pillows and he had burst out laughing. "Yes Mama," he said with a grin.

Now he was back there again. The more time he spent with her the more he realized that he could not bear to be away from her. It was killing him to leave her each evening and go to his apartment.

"So ask her to marry you." Tyler suggested sensibly. They were in his office going over the financial reports.

"What?" Marcus' mind had been far away, barely taking in what his friend had been saying. He was supposed to be taking her to dinner later but he was not sure he should; maybe he should cancel.

"Ask her to marry you Marcus." His friend repeated patiently. "You have been going around like a bear with a sorehead for the past several weeks and we know the cause of it."

"She is not ready yet," he said broodingly, turning over the paperweight in his hands. He had thought of asking her several times but she had shied away from any discussions of the future. He knew if he forced her hand she would not see him again. He could not risk that.

"Have you asked her?" Tyler put aside the document and gave him his full attention. He had seen his friend go from the confident cocky womanizer to one who walked around like a love sick teenager and he could not help but smile at the wonder of it all.

"No," Marcus said with a short laugh. "But I know she is not ready yet. She cried in my arms about the bastard that died in that crash and what he had done to her!" He curled his hand around the paperweight and Tyler thanked God that the guy was already dead. "I find myself wondering if she is still in love with the son of a bitch."

"So ask her and stop torturing yourself wondering about it." Tyler told him practically.

"What if it is an answer I don't want to hear?" Marcus countered.

"What if it is?"

"I think I will give her a break for a few days." Marcus told him.

"Your choice man, but ask yourself if that is going to make the situation better or worse."

*****

It made it worse. He had called her and told her he had a meeting to go into so he would not make dinner. She had sounded disappointed, causing his heart to soar in hope and then he had stayed away for two whole days but how he suffered. He could not function at work and he could not sleep at night. He kept taking up the phone to call her and putting it down back.

Kaila had called him and asked if he could come over but he had told her no. He had not seen her since he met Donna and he had no interest in rekindling whatever it was they had.

"Are you sure?" she purred, her voice getting on his nerves. "I am totally naked underneath my robe and I am craving your penis right now."

"Kaila I am not in the mood," he had told her abruptly, wanting to get off the phone with her, somehow feeling as if he was cheating on Donna, which was ridiculous of course.

"Oh so I have been replaced?" she asked angrily, the purr gone from her voice.

"We were never in that kind of a relationship for you to think you have been replaced." He told her mildly.

Without another word she disconnected the call and he gave a sigh of relief. Now back to his current situation, he thought moodily. He had not called her and she had not called him either. What was that telling him?

*****

Donna missed him. She did not think it was possible but she did. Not hearing from him was making her spin in circles and was making her miserable. She hated feeling this way. She did not want to think about him so much but she could not help it. She wished she could go where he was or even call and demanded that he come and see her but she had to stand her ground. She was a child of God and she had to let him be her guide. That meant playing by the rules. If she went to him she knew what was going to happen.

"Honey, do you want to come and help me put some frosting on this cake?" her mother called out to her. She was in her bedroom being miserable and she supposed it was time she stopped.

"Coming Mom," she called out. She had come home for the evening and had felt tired but had been looking forward to seeing Marcus.

"Ah there you are honey would you pass me the piping bag please?" she had a large cake on the cake stand. "Millicent's daughter is having a birthday party tomorrow afternoon at her school and the child insists on having me bake a cake for her, as if I don't have enough to do." Lydia grumbled good-naturedly. "How are you?"

"I am fine," Donna said with a forced smile, taking a seat on one of the stools in the small homely kitchen. She had sat in this very spot when she was a little girl and watched her mother bake pies or whatever else she made.

"That young man Marcus seems to be very interested in you." Her mother commented, not looking up from the designs she was making on the cake.

"I suppose he is." Donna wished her mother had not brought him up, missing him was becoming like a permanent ache inside her.

"Are you interested in him?" the question was asked casually but Donna knew it was a loaded one.

"I think I am," she said carefully.

"You have been through a lot but that does not escape the fact that life has a way of giving us another chance and maybe the second chance we get is really the first one and the supposed first one was just a smoke screen." Lydia put down the instrument she had been using and looked at her beautiful daughter. "The Lord puts people in our way. They either bring us down or help us up. Whatever they do, it should be a lesson for us to learn. Marcus, I think, is a positive lesson for you to learn so do not let the negative lessons you experienced deflect from the positive one." She reached for her daughter's hands on the counter. "Explore your feelings honey and if he is the one, grab him with both hands and let God lead you."

*****

He took her out to dinner the following evening. At first she thought about telling him no but she wanted to see him. When he picked her up at seven she did not ask where he had been for two days, after all she had her pride.

He had told her to dress formally and she was wearing an emerald green dress that shimmered and swirled around her legs when she walked. She had tiny emerald earrings in her lobes and a silver chain with a matching pendant. The dress had thin spaghetti straps and she put on a short black jacket over it because the time was getting cold.

He took her hand and led her out to the car. A white Mercedes Benz with chrome rims. "Do you think you have enough vehicles?" she asked him dryly as she secured the seatbelt.

"I am not going to apologize or feel guilty about living the way I do," he told her quietly as he drove off. He was wearing a dark blue jacket with a light blue shirt and a red tie. "I give a lot back and I went through life without a lot of things. I just want to enjoy some of what life has to offer now." He paused and glanced at her briefly. "I hope that does not change anything between us, Donna. I am not shallow and I know these are just things and they are replaceable, not like people."

"I am happy you realize that." She told him.

He looked at her for a moment. As usual she was looked as beautiful as a forbidden art. 'Mount Everest' his friend Tyler had called her but when he touched her she had melted into him. How does he get past what she had been through? How can he convince her that he would never knowingly hurt her?

The restaurant was a high profile one and for a minute Donna held back, the unpleasant memories assailing her. "We can turn back and go to the crab place if you want," he told her quietly, feeling her resistance.

She took a deep breath and smiled. "I am okay, thanks." She told him gratefully.

He was known by the manager of course and he was greeted by several people. Donna saw a few actresses and actors and an up and coming singer. She also saw the curious gazes and knew that she was recognized. She thought she would have felt ashamed and intimidated when this moment came but she felt a peace settling over her and she relaxed. Their table was way in the corner and gave them privacy.

"A basketball buddy of mine owns the place." Marcus told her as soon as they were seated and the menu brought to them. The ambiance was magnificent and there was sports memorabilia all over on the walls but instead of looking crass it fit into the atmosphere.

"Really?" she teased, her dark brown eyes twinkling.

Marcus' breath caught in his throat as he looked at her. How on earth did he stay away from her for two whole days? He thought grimly.

"I can't stay away from you." He told her abruptly, putting the menu away. He already knew what he wanted, the lobster in lemon juice. "I tried because I did not want to overwhelm you with what I am feeling but I cannot stay away."

"So you were deliberately avoiding me?" she asked him coolly. "I am not into games Marcus; I have been down that road before."

"Please don't do that," he said with quiet steel in his voice.

"Do what?"

"Don't compare me to him. You keep doing that Donna and I don't deserve it. I am me. I am Marcus Wellington, not that creep that let you down. I hate what he did to you and I hate that you color me the same way."

"I don't think you are the same." She told him, leaning forward earnestly. "I have to sort out things in my head and it has nothing to do with you."

"It has everything to do with me!" he hissed. He settled back against the seat as the Maitre D approached to take their order.

They ate in silence, each caught up in their own thoughts and looked up when someone came up to their table. "Marcus! I thought that was you."

His heart sank as he realized who it was. He and Serena had been an item a year ago and for a while he and everyone else had thought it would have led to something permanent. She was a swimsuit model who had graced the covers of some of the biggest magazines.

"Serena," he stood up and hugged her briefly. "This is Donna-"

He did not get to finish as the girl finished the sentence. "Brown. We were in the same profession." Serena extended a hand gracefully. "Sorry about what happened to you."

"Thank you." Donna took her hand, feeling the jealousy going through her. She had seen their pictures in the papers together as soon as she had started doing her research on Marcus and knew they had been an item.

"Darling how have you been doing?" she turned her large dark brown eyes back on Marcus. She was strikingly attractive with curly black hair and a cocoa brown complexion that was so smooth it defied description. She had on her signature bright red lipstick and her talon like nails were of the same color.

"Very well, thank you." Marcus said formally, feeling very uncomfortable.

"I am in town for a few days, it would be nice if you would give me a call. I am staying at the apartment." With a graceful nod at Donna and an intimate smile at Marcus she walked away with swaying hips.

The silence after her departure was palpable and Marcus was afraid to say anything to her.

"Say something," he said after awhile as they continued to eat in silence.

"Like what?" Donna hated that she was feeling so insecure.

"Like asking me what she was to me." He willed her to look at him.

"It's not my concern," she told him with a shrug.

"To hell it's not," he said harshly, his voice low. "She was someone I cared deeply about and at one point we thought it would go somewhere. I am not going to that apartment Donna; I can assure you of that."

"You are an adult Marcus and you can do whatever you please," she forced herself to be cool and collected. "You can see anyone you want to see or be with. We are not exclusive after all."

"Damn you Donna," he said quietly and Donna looked at him startled. "No matter what I do I will be the bad guy. I am just a stereotypical black guy who's intent is having as many women as I can. Aren't you going to ask me if I have a baby mama or two stashed away somewhere?" he asked her bitterly.

"Do you?" she asked him with a tapered eyebrow raised.

He sat there looking at her, his heart drowning inside him. He was not going to win; he realized that; despair flooding through him. The guy was dead but it was as if he was still here sitting at the table with them and he could not compete with a dead guy. He would have stood a chance if he was alive but he was dead and he could not compete; he was losing. "I will take you home."

He drove in silence and she had too much pride to say anything either. She knew she had gone too far but maybe it was for the best. She had seen the predatory look on the girl's face and felt all the old feelings from the past coming back. She did not belong to that world, not anymore and he did.

He dropped her off and waited until she had gone inside and then he drove off without a backward look.

*****

"You need to call her," Tyler looked at his friend in sympathy. He had seen his friend go from being a confident happy go lucky dude to one who had become withdrawn and unhappy.

"I can't," Marcus said abruptly, using the towel to wipe the sweat dripping from his face. It had been two days since he had seen her or spoken to her and he felt as if he was dying slowly.

It was Friday after work, he and Tyler were working out in the gym. There were several other employees there as well. He still had to approve of the new sportswear they were planning to put on the market but so far he had not been able to concentrate on anything. He was not sleeping well and he barely ate. "I cannot fight what she has going on with her and I am tired bro," he sat down heavily on the bench they lay on to press weights.

"What's the alternative?" Tyler asked him, putting away the weights he had been using. "You walking around unhappy and barking at everyone. Letting your company be neglected? What's the worst that can happen?"

"You're joking right?" Marcus looked at him incredulously. "I am in love with her so that means my heart is involved. What's the worst that can happen? I am losing my sanity because I am in love with a woman who cannot get past what happened to her in the past. I don't know, maybe it's karma." He said bitterly. "I have used women in the past so maybe this is my pay back."

"Maybe," his friend agreed, grinning as Marcus looked up at him sharply. "But God does not go on punishing forever. You need to pray about it my brother and let God show you what to do."

"I have not prayed in so long," Marcus looked away in contemplation.

"Maybe it's time you start."

*****

"My dear how lovely to see you at a prayer meeting!" Jessica exclaimed as Donna took her seat in the middle row. Her mother was still outside discussing something with Sister Monica about the Sunday school department.

"I have been here a few times before Sister Jessica." Donna said with a smile as the woman took a seat beside her.

"I know my dear. It's always so lovely to see you."

It was her husband Michael who was conducting the study and they were doing the book of Job.

"Job's friends formed a supposed bond of support around him but they in fact made things worse by feeding him a lot of negative vibes." Michael told the class in a serious tone. "There are times when we need people the most but that's when they let us down but God never does and we need to always remember that."

There was a lively discussion that followed and although she did not participate, Donna listened avidly. She had been in a state of numbness over the past two days. She kept telling herself that it was better it was over before it really began. It was best that she found out how things were before she got seriously involved. But no amount of praying for peace and contentment was working. She was miserable and she spent the nights in her bedroom crying. Her mother had not asked her anything about Marcus but she had seen her looking at her curiously. She was not yet ready to share.

She stood up with the rest of the congregation as they sang 'All to Jesus I surrender' and closed her eyes in prayer as she sang the hymn. She was determined to put him out of her mind and concentrate on her life now. She and Marcus had not meant to be together and that was all there was to it.

Chapter 6

Donna got the news when she was at home one night just as she was getting ready to go to bed. It had been a week since she had heard from Marcus and even though she thought of him constantly, she had stopped crying. His mother had called and said she wanted her to come over but she had made some excuse because she was not sure she could go and be with someone so close to him; at least not yet.

Her phone rang when she was just about to put on her nightgown. "Hello?" she answered uncertainly wondering who could be calling her at this hour.

"Is this Donna?" it was a male voice.

"Yes this is she," she answered. "Who is this?"

"My name is Tyler and I am a friend of Marcus'; he is in the hospital." The man continued.

Donna started trembling. No! Her mind screamed. Please God not again!

"He was involved in a car crash," the voice continued as if from far away. She wanted to call out for her mother to help her but she could not find the voice. "He is unconscious but he was calling for you. Can you come over?"

"Where is he?" she heard herself asking.

He told her and she hung up the phone. She turned around to see her mother standing in the doorway. "You heard?" she asked quietly coming further into the room. She was pale and she just stood there as if she did not know what to do next.

"His mother called a little while ago. Get dressed honey I will drive." Lydia said softly, her heart breaking at the look on her daughter's face.

It was déjà vu all over again and this time it was worse because of the way she felt about Marcus even though she had seen her trying to deny her feelings. "God is in charge darling." She continued as the girl took out a pair of denims and a dark blue sweater. It had been raining earlier and it had gotten chilly. Donna nodded. She did not want to think; she did not want to feel and the blessed numbness had come over her.

*****

They got to the hospital in record time and his mother was already there. She saw a young man hovering over her and she suspected that it was the same person who had called her. Lydia took her daughter's hand and led her over to where they were.

"Honey I am so glad you are here," Marla greeted her as she came over. She was no longer in a wheelchair but was walking with a cane. "This is Marcus' best friend Tyler. He was the one who called you."

"How is he?" she gripped the woman's hands tightly as if seeking a lifeline.

"He has a concussion and he has been slipping in and out of consciousness for the past few hours." Marla told her.

"Sorry to meet you under these circumstances Donna, I have heard a lot about you and of course I have always admired your pictures," Tyler told her with a smile. "He was on his way to see you and the car slid on the wet road. Marcus drives too fast."

"He was on his way to see me?" Donna's hands trembled as she held on to his mother.

"Honey, we serve a great big wonderful God!" the woman assured her with a smile. "The doctor said he was lucky but I told him that luck had nothing to do with it. God did."

Just then the doctor came out and everyone turned to face him. "He is awake," the man told them with a smile. "He is asking for Donna, is she here?"

"Yes," Donna released his mother's hand and turned around to look at her.

"Go," the woman urged with a smile. "He needs you."

The bandage looked especially white against his dark skin but apart from that he looked okay and as soon as she came inside he held out his hand for her to take. "It takes me being in the hospital to get you to come to me," he teased in a low voice, pulling her down on the bed beside him.

"You almost died," she whispered, pulling her hand away from him, her eyes wide and frightened. "You could have died," she was gripping the white cotton sheets that were on the bed.

With a sinking heart he realized that she had gone right back to the horrible experience she had had before.

"Baby look at me," he told her urgently, ignoring the pounding in his head. He had to get through to her. "I am okay. I am all in one piece."

She could not see him. All she saw was the lights coming towards her and waking up in the hospital and now he was here; he was in the hospital. "Donna please baby," his voice sounded far away and it took him shaking her for her to realize that he was calling her name and pleading with her. "Baby I am sorry please forgive me; if it will make you feel better I promise I will never drive again, please Donna. Oh God please," his voice was desperate and it was like he was praying which indeed he was.

She looked down at him and he finally got through to her. With a soft anguished cry, she dropped her head on his chest and curled her hands into the hospital gown he had on and the tears came. He held her to him, his own tears coming as he heard the anguish she was letting out. He had been coming to see her and he was driving too fast in his haste to be with her.

He had let a week pass and he had not spoken to her nor seen her and he realized that Tyler was right, he was not doing well without her. Even if he had to tie her down she was going to listen to him. He shuddered to think he had almost lost his life and he had put her through misery again.

"I seem to have this habit of crying into your clothes," her voice, husky with emotion mumbled into his chest and he closed his eyes in relief. She sounded better.

"That's what I am here for," he told her hoarsely, easing her up to look at him. Her face was tear streaked and she was not wearing a stitch of make-up. She still was the most beautiful woman he had ever seen in his life. He used his fingers to wipe away her tears. "I promise that whenever you cry again it will be tears of joy or of pleasure when I am making love to you and we will be crying together."

"I missed you," she told him softly, holding his hands and not caring what happened next. "I thought it was better if we did not see each other again but I have missed you so much that I could not sleep and I was miserable all the time."

He cupped her face in his hands. "I could not eat and I could not function and a very good friend of mine advised me to go to you and not to leave until you agreed to be my wife." He felt as she went still. "I want to marry you Donna because I love you and I do not want to live without you. I don't care how long it takes for you to get over what he did to you; I will do whatever it takes if you'll say yes you will marry me."

Donna's lips trembled as she looked at him. She loved him; there was no doubt about that and seeing him here like this, lying in a hospital bed only confirmed that God had given her a second chance and this time she was not going to blow it. "I would love to be your wife," she told him huskily.

"And that's a yes?" he held her tightly, his heart hammering inside his chest.

"It's a yes," she told him with a heart stopping smile.

He gave a whoop that had the nurses and doctors running inside the room. "How soon can I get out of here doc? This absolutely beautiful and amazing woman just agreed to marry me!"

*****

He was released the following day and he refused to let Donna leave his hospital bed. "In case you go home and change your mind." He told her seriously. His mother and hers and Tyler were told the news and after a short visit they left the couple alone to celebrate together.

"I don't want a very big wedding," she told him as she snuggled up to him on the bed, her head on his chest. "I know we cannot escape that but I don't want it to turn out to be a circus."

"It's going to be difficult but I will see what I can do." He told her softly, holding her tightly against him. The papers had already made much of his accident and he was sure they were going to make much of his engagement to a former super model as well. He was aware of how camera shy she had become and would try to shield her from the vultures.

*****

The engagement party was held at his mother's place. It was too cold to have it outdoors so it was kept in the living room. Marla Wellington could not stop smiling and when Donna arrived in an ice pink dress that molded her stunning figure, she felt as if she was looking at an angel. The girl was absolutely beautiful. Marcus held her close to him and he had given her a ten carat diamond ring with emeralds all around it.

The place was teeming with people and he had told her he had tried to control the amount of people who came but he had not been able to.

"It's okay," she told him, her smile revealing the cute space between her teeth. "I am actually getting used to all the attention."

The night turned out to be beautiful and he stood up and gave a speech. "I met my match when I met Donna," he looked down at her, his eyes holding hers. It was like they were the only two people in the room. "I never thought I could feel this way about another person and I met you and I fell hard. I love you my baby, my woman, my heart and I will always love you." Donna stood up and went into his arms.

"Your woman?" she whispered against his ear.

"I had to say it," he whispered back. He held her face between his hands and bent his head taking her lips in a gentle devastating kiss.

*****

They were married on Thanksgiving Day. He had offered to get her a wedding planner but she had declined. "I want to plan my own wedding." She had told him with a whimsical smile. She still had trouble with him driving and it killed them both to be away from each other.

Each time he took her out and brought her back to her mother's place it was like hell. For the week leading up to the wedding he did not come to see her, he only called and even then it was pure torture.

"My bed is too big without you in it," he had told her with a groan.

"Maybe we should not be talking about beds," she had told him softly. She had been lying in bed with the phone at her ear. They talked to each other every night before going to bed.

"Even if we don't talk about it we are still thinking about it." He commented huskily.

"So let's stop talking altogether," she teased him.

"That's not an option." He had told her firmly.

*****

It was their wedding day. Marcus had held his breath for the last two months because he had been afraid that maybe she would back out when it came nearer to the day. But here she was, walking up the aisle on the arms of Pastor Michael who had asked her to be the giveaway father.

The congregation held their collective breaths as she made her way slowly towards him. She was beautiful. Her dress hugged her slender curvaceous figure and fell in graceful folds down to her ankles. The bodice was held up by two very thin straps embedded with tiny diamonds and her hair was lightly teased and had white rosebuds at one side. She was wearing diamond drop earrings and a single tier diamond that fell into her cleavage.

The papers referred to her as the snow queen and raved about her beauty. "Ms. Donna Brown-Wellington could have continued her career as an international model. She is even more beautiful now than she was back then." One writer said.

Another one caught her as she laughed up at her new husband as they were walking out of the church. "A laugh that should be bottled and sold" was the caption.

She had moved her clothes to Marcus' apartment the day before and was setting foot in there for the first time. She had been determined to keep her innocence and although it had been hard on him, he had respected her wishes and so they had made the decision for her to stay away from his place.

He lifted her across the threshold and only put her down when they reached the bedroom. She had caught a glimpse of all his awards and ribbons hanging over the huge fireplace. "Should I be shivering in awe of your many trophies and fame?" she teased him as he placed her on the bed.

"The only shivering I want is when I am inside you," he told her huskily. She looked up at him; his handsome chocolate brown face. He had taken off his white jacket and was in his white shirt, with two buttons undone. "I love you so much it is hard for me to say it with words."

"Tell me with your body," she whispered, feeling the fire starting inside her.

He undressed her, taking his time with the zipper of her lovely dress. She stepped out of it, revealing the startlingly white lace camisole that clung to her and outlined her every curve. He undressed hastily and climbed on the bed beside her. Donna trembled slightly. She had seen his erection and had felt a slight fear go through her; he was too big. She thought.

"I won't hurt you," he correctly gauged her reaction. "I will take my time even though I want you so much that I am shaking from the need." He took off the garment slowly, his eyes smoldering as he took in her small breasts with the dusky brown nipples that had gone as hard as pebbles.

He kissed her, his touch gentle and his mouth hungry. She clasped her hands around his neck as she opened her mouth beneath his. Marcus was not sure he could not wait; he felt his control slipping away from him and the desperation for her taking over. He had to have her now and damn finesse. He dragged his mouth away from hers and ran his hands over her breasts, his mouth following as he took a nipple between his teeth, using his tongue to lick and taste her. Donna gasped and arched her body closer to him; she was trembling from the need of him.

"Marcus," she called his name huskily as he went to her other nipple, pulling it inside his mouth hungrily.

He wanted to discover her entire body but his desire would not let him. He felt as if a fire had been lit inside his body and he was being burned alive. He had to have her now. He released her nipple and came over her. He entered her slowly, straining not to give in to the demands of his body. He gritted his teeth as he met upon her barrier and he pushed against it, his eyes holding hers, his hands holding her hips gently. Before she knew what he was doing, he captured her lips the same time he pushed past the breach and entered her fully, capturing her cry of pain inside his mouth. He stayed still inside her waiting until her body had become accustomed to his length.

He moved when she did, his mouth still on hers as his thrusts became more urgent. Donna felt the fire licking through her body as she dug her fingers into his muscled shoulders. She clasped him around his waist and lifted her body to get even closer to him, moving with him in perfect harmony, her mouth clinging to his and increasing the pace when he did. The soreness between her legs already forgotten as the pleasure of him being inside her flooded her body as she felt his soul touched hers.

They came together violently like waves crashing against the sand. Their cries mingled together as did the tears as he emptied himself inside her. His hands gripped her as his seed spilled inside her and she gave herself to him like she had never done before. He was shivering as he held her body close to him.

It was a long time before they drifted back down to earth and they talked.

She told him about her painful past. "I always suspected that he was seeing someone else but when I asked him he was always denying it and calling me paranoid so I dropped it. But I could hear the whispered phone calls when he thought I was not listening and when we went out together, I swear I felt eyes boring into my back." His hand drifted between her legs and he touched her there. "Marcus I can't talk when you do that." She moaned, biting her lip as his fingers slipped inside her.

"I have to touch you so please bear with me." He worked his fingers inside her, watching her face as he did so. She looked like raw sex and he felt himself hardening again. "I don't want to talk or hear about him, I want to kill him with my bare hands because of what he did to you. He hurt you and nobody does that, it's unacceptable."

He spread the lips of her vagina and ran his fingers between the folds. Donna felt it again. The fire burning through her. "I love you," he mumbled as he climbed back on top of her and entered her forcefully, lifting her legs high as he thrust inside her over and over again. Donna sobbed out his name and with an intense expression on his face he thrust inside her making her feel the length of him, his body shuddering as he came inside her. He pulled out just a little bit then plunging into her again and again as she came all over him.

She slept on top of him, her hands curled on his chest and he stroked her back and looked up at the high brown ceiling that was in his bedroom. He had wanted to crawl inside her and not come back out. She was his wife and he did not know what he had done to deserve her. His mother had told him that God had provided her for him and he had better not blow it. He smiled as he remembered how happy she had been as they had announced their engagement. "She is beautiful son and not only outside because you know I don't care about that but she has an inside beauty that is hard to find, so please cherish her."

She did not have to say that to him; he already knew what he had and he intended to treat her the way she deserved to be treated.

"You're supposed to be the sleeping," she murmured into his chest.

"I can't sleep because I keep wanting to sink myself deep inside you." He told her huskily. She had lifted her head and was looking at him.

"You're insatiable," she said softly, one finger tracing his bottom lip. He caught her finger between his teeth and started nibbling which started a sensation inside her.

"Only for you," he reached down and positioned her so that she was sitting on him, his penis deep inside her. "See what I mean?" he moved inside her slowly. "Are you tired?"

"Not anymore," she told him with a gasp. She braced her hands against his chest and matched his thrusts with hers. "I am on fire for you!" she gasped and moving her head she claimed his lips with hers.

Chapter 7

He took a week off from the office because he wanted to spend time with her and to show her around. He took her to his office building the first day and introduced her to his staff and kept saying 'my wife'.

"I think they know already that I am your wife," she told him in amusement as he stopped in his office so that he could sign some papers before they left.

"I am saying it for my benefit," he told her ruefully, pulling her into his arms and kissing her lips gently. They had woke up at about eleven this morning completely naked and he had made love to her again. He fixed her breakfast in between kissing her and running his hands all over her body. She had enjoyed the entire experience immensely.

He showed her the basketball court and the gym and the new sportswear that he still had not approved yet. "I like the feel of it but I don't know yet. What do you think?"

She held up the bright gold and green sleeveless shirt and the matching leggings. And felt the fabric. "I love the feel of the material and the style is not bad."

"But?" he asked her shrewdly.

"I think it would be better if the neckline was changed." She told him. "I'll try it on and let you know better what I think."

"Not now though, we have things to see. We are actually on our honeymoon so let's get out of here." He pulled her along with him.

*****

He took her to a hot dog stand where they ordered the biggest hot dogs the vendor could make and went to sit on a bench to eat them. It was approaching Christmas and the lights were already decorating buildings and business places and there was a Red Cross man at a store front ringing his bell. It was freezing cold and even though they dressed warm, the cold still managed to seep through.

They went to a small café that was empty at that time of the day and had hot chocolate. He told her about his childhood and growing up without a father.

"I had resentment growing up because I thought to myself that if I had a father around then our lives would not be so hard," he automatically leaned forward and wiped whipped cream from the side of her lips. Her face was glowing from the cold and something else he would like to think had to do with him. "I said it to my mother one time and she sat me down and told me that I had a father and his name is Jesus and he is the ultimate father. She told me that not having a father figure in my life should not alter God's plans for my life. She said that I can be anything I wanted to be if I just believe in myself and she did not want to hear me feeling sorry for myself ever again."

"What a woman!" Donna said softly. "She gave it something that was priceless. She gave you a reason to succeed and to hold on to while you were doing so."

"And I love her for it." He said quietly. "She believed in me and that let me believe in myself."

"You know what?" Donna asked suddenly.

"What?" he said in amusement looking at her animated face.

"Let's go home, I want to play housewife for a little bit and fix you supper, sit on the couch and watch television like a newly married couple." She told him.

"Sounds like a good idea." He pulled some cash from his wallet and put it on the table and taking her hand, they left.

*****

"I had no idea you could cook," Marcus tasted the stew simmering on the stove. His apartment was ultra modern and he often referred to it as his bachelor pad. It was far from being plain with its bold red and black design and three bedrooms with two baths and a front and back porch.

"My mother insisted I learned even though I hated the kitchen I was more intent on gazing at the beautiful women in fashion magazines and wishing I was them." She was chopping up vegetables deftly and he stole a piece of carrot from the cutting board.

"And you became one of them." He commented, sitting on a stool beside her. She had taken off her winter gear and put on knee length shorts and a sleeveless T-shirt that showed her nipples. He had been sucking on them earlier when they came home and she had pushed him away reluctantly saying that if they continued then she would not be able to show him her culinary skills.

"I have a proposition." He added and waited until she looked at him. "How do you feel about taking over the department that designs the sportswear for the company?"

"Don't you already have someone who does that?" she asked him curiously.

"Not really," he said with a shrug. "I come up with the ideas sometimes and sometimes it's Tyler but we have not been able to pin down someone who is good at this and it's a fairly new department, which is not really a department yet so we were just playing it by ear. So what do you say?"

"Working with my husband?" she tapped a finger against her lip as if considering. "What are my remuneration packages? Do I get health benefits and a company car?"

He grabbed her around the waist and set her own on his lap. "All of that and more," he told her huskily. "Everything I have belongs to you." He took her lips with his and plundered her mouth, his tongue delving inside and dueling with hers. He released her lips but only to pull the shirt over her head, revealing her breasts, their nipples already hardened from his touch. He took a nipple inside his mouth and pulled on it causing her to gasp and arch her back against the counter. He moved to the next and his tongue licked and teased her until she felt as if she could not bear it any more. He lifted her and put her on the counter and pulled off her shorts and panties parting her legs and pulling her to the edge.

"Marcus," she gasped as he bent his head and touched her mound with his tongue. Donna cried out sharply, her hands gripping the edge of the counter. When his tongue plunged inside her she almost passed out at the unbelievable pleasure. His tongue delved further inside her, exploring every inch of her. She was sobbing and begging him for release when he pulled out of her. He dragged his shorts off; he pulled her down on him, entering her quickly and holding her against him as he thrust inside her.

"I can't get enough of you," he told her hoarsely holding her hips steady as he thrust inside her and stopped, looking at her passion filled face. "I want to go so deep that I find it difficult to come back out, I need you Donna," he pushed inside her and stumbled back against the stool, thrusting into her rapidly.

Donna clung to him and moved her body frantically over him, her control long gone as she rode him relentlessly. He shot his load inside her with a hoarse cry, holding onto her as her release came right after his. He took her mouth and swallowed her frantic cries as they rode the waves together.

*****

She took up the position and an office was provided for her with her name on the door and a title: 'Director of Sporting Gear' which she told him sounded weird.

She worked closely with the designer to fix the problem on the sportswear and Marcus asked her if she would model it. "What?" she had looked at him startled.

They were standing in her newly established office and she was sitting behind her large oak desk looking at some designs she had been given. They had spent the rest of the week at home barely going anywhere, but visiting their mothers and going to church. They had spent the time exploring each other's bodies and getting to know the other by talking a lot.

"I know you said you were never getting back into that life again but hear me out," he came and sat on the edge of her desk facing her. He was wearing dark blue pants, a silver gray shirt and a thick red cashmere sweater. He looked like a model for sportswear. His simple gold wedding band that he never took off even when he was in the shower, glistened in the light overhead. "You would be doing the modeling exclusively for the company and you would be showcasing the clothes you help design. How about it?"

She had to admit it sounded like an excellent idea. But going in front of a camera again? "What if I freeze up?" she said uncertainly.

"You won't," he assured her. "But to be certain I want us to pray about it first."

She looked at him in surprise. She had not tried to push her Christianity on him. She had noticed when she was reading her Bible, he would come sit beside her and read with her and when she was praying he would join her. "I think that's an excellent idea." She told him softly with a smile and they stood right there in her office and did just that.

*****

"How do you feel?" Lionel the photographer asked her with a smile. He was the best there was and Marcus had wanted the best.

"Like I should have said no," Donna said ruefully. The gear molded her body like a second skin and she had to admit that it felt good against her body.

"You'll do great," he told her. They were doing the shoot in the gym which had been set up to accommodate them. Her make-up was flawless and barely discernible.

She did different shots. One with her lifting two pound weights and one with her with a basketball in her hands and another with her holding a tennis racket. There was also one with her sitting on the grass with her legs drawn up to her chest and a brilliant smile on her face.

Marcus watched her from the shadows of the doorway because he had promised her he would not be present in case he made her nervous but he could not resist coming to see her. She was a professional and no matter what she said, she was made for this.

"She is truly beautiful isn't she?" Tyler said beside him. He had been so engrossed in looking at her that he had not noticed that his best friend had come up beside him.

"She is," he admitted quietly. "It is quite okay for me to be sneaking peeks at my wife but it certainly is not for you to do so." He told his friend bluntly.

"A lot of men are going to drooling over her when the magazine comes out so I am going to see what you are going to do when that happens." Tyler looked at him in amusement. "Planning to buy out the entire publication?"

"Had not thought about that," Marcus muttered, turning to look back at her as she laughed at something Lionel said. His body tensed as he saw the photographer touch her chin to position her face correctly.

"Get a grip bro, your jealousy is showing." Tyler told him dryly as he saw his reaction. "That woman loves you and she is a professional, don't let her see your insecurities."

*****

The magazine came out just before Christmas and it was an instant success. It was sold out by the first week and Donna Brown-Wellington became what she had never wanted to be again: a much sought after model. The photo on the front page was said to be the best of the bunch; the one with her sitting on the grassy knoll smiling brightly at the camera. As the papers put it: 'Donna Brown-Wellington redefines sports in a new way. With that smile of hers she makes all of us want to get fit.' She turned down all the offers and told them that she had an exclusive contract with Wellington Sports.

"Are you sure?" Marcus asked her as she turned down yet another lucrative offer.

"Positive," she told him firmly. They were in her office and she was in the middle of working with the designer to come up with a line of sportswear for women on the go. "I have what I need right here and I told you definitely that I have no intention of getting involved in that again. I have two relationships that mean the world to me: My relationship with God and my marriage and I have no intention of putting anything before that."

"I thought now that you are famous again you would not have time for poor little me," he teased her.

"That will never happen," she told him huskily, walking into his arms and looping her hands around his neck. "What would I do without the incredible lovemaking you have introduced me to?"

"Nice to know my body is of some use to you." He told her throatily as he claimed her lips in a tender heart racing kiss.

*****

They went to their parents' homes for Christmas. They spent Christmas Eve with her mother and Christmas day with his mother even though they were back and forth from the two houses.

"Honey you look radiant!" Lydia greeted them at the door, giving her a kiss and hugging her tall handsome son in law fondly. "I see you are taking care of my daughter Marcus."

"She takes care of me," he said sending his wife a wicked glance.

"We take care of each other," she said sending him a telling look. "Mom the house smells like fruit cake and pie."

"I have orders to deliver as we speak. I am so happy you are here now and not later. I am afraid I am going to turn you into a delivery person Marcus."

"No problem," he said easily, putting down their bags and following her into the kitchen. "Just let me know where and I am at your service."

"Bless you son." Lydia said with a beaming smile.

They were both put to work and given instructions as to what to do and before long all the orders had been filled. "Thank goodness you came and honey, I am so proud of you. Those pictures in the magazine are so lovely I had to cut them out and frame every one of them. I have them in the living room above the fireplace."

"I hadn't noticed." Donna exclaimed going into the living room to look. "You are as bad as Marcus," she said with a smile, looking at the framed pictures hanging on the wall. "He has his in his den and he looks at them all the time."

"I don't blame him." Lydia told her.

They had dinner in the kitchen and Lydia caught them up with the latest news around the community. Donna could not believe that it had been barely a month since she had left her mother's house. They had been back for church but had not stayed and she found herself looking around to see if the place was still the same.

Later that night in her bedroom, way after eleven o'clock, after they had put their presents underneath the tree in the living room, Marcus held her in his arms. He had not made love to her and tonight he just felt like holding her.

"I used to spend so much time in this room after Mom and Dad had gone to bed praying to God for a brother or a sister so that I could have someone to play with," she told him with a laugh.

"And when the years passed and there was no answer to your prayer you wondered why God was being so mean to you." He said shrewdly.

"How did you know?" she raised her head and rested her arms on his naked chest. He never slept in anything and even though he asked her not to, she still was not comfortable enough to follow suit.

"I used to pray and ask for a brother specifically so that we could beat up people together," he grinned at her sheepishly. Her face was devoid of make-up and scrubbed clean and she looked like a teenager. "I was teased at school a lot about my raggedy ass clothes and the fact that my mother was a household helper."

"Look at you now." She told him softly. "I love you Marcus Wellington," she whispered.

"You haven't said that to me in a while," he told her huskily. "I love you too my wife." He spent the rest of the night showing her how much.

*****

They woke up very early on Christmas morning to flurries. They hurriedly got dressed and went outside in the yard to catch the soft snowflakes in their hands. Lydia stood by the window watching them a smile on her lips. She saw her daughter run off and her husband catch her in a hug. They stood there in the falling snow in a passionate embrace. To God be the glory, she thought, moving away and efficiently piling the stack of chocolate chip pancakes with a touch of cinnamon on the table. There was homemade eggnog in a bowl in the center and eggs and bacon there, also a steaming pot of coffee and a jug of orange juice.

"This is the best breakfast I have had in a long time," Marcus said patting his flat stomach and eyeing his wife.

"Be careful what you say, I just might have to leave you here," Donna warned him as she drank down her orange juice.

They gave Lydia the gifts they had brought her. She exclaimed over the different colored house gowns and the quality of them, the expensive winter coat and baking accessories Donna had given her. Marcus had bought her perfume and a lovely gold watch that shone in the light. "God bless you both," she said with tears in her eyes.

They went over to his mother's house in the afternoon because they, along with her mother, were having Christmas dinner there.

"The Lord be praised!" Marla Wellington greeted them with hugs and tears in her eyes. She had stopped using her cane and was getting progressively better. "Lydia, I see you all the time but these two I don't get to see often." The house was decorated all over with Christmas decorations and there were lights everywhere.

"Who on earth did all these things for you mom?" Marcus asked her looking around the house at the myriads of lights and other decorations.

"Some people from church. I have a reason to celebrate Christmas this year, my son and my daughter were coming to spend it with me." She told them.

They sat in the living room where there was a fire blazing in the hearth. They were served hot chocolate and the pie that Lydia had brought over.

Marla told them how happy she was for both of them. "I thank God the day he sent you over here to help me Donna and I knew you were the right woman for my son." She beamed at them. Marcus had eventually told Donna how his mother had wanted them to be together from the beginning.

"So am I," Donna told her softly looking at her husband, their eyes holding each other's. the two mothers looked at each other with smiles and slowly left the room.

"I never showed you the trophy room," he told her softly reaching for her hand.

"No, you never did," she said as she went with him.

His bedroom was still the way he left it when he went away with all his sports paraphernalia and huge posters of him on the wall when he had been playing basketball. "Mom kept everything and every write up I ever got, she kept the clippings."

"I don't blame her," Donna murmured looking up at the life sized poster. He was standing behind her and closed his arms around her waist. She leaned back against him with a sigh, contentment washing over her. "I want our children to know the accomplishments of their father."

He went still at her words and turned her around to face him. "What are you saying?" he asked her huskily.

She looped her hands around his neck. "I am saying my darling husband, that I think I am pregnant."

Chapter 8

He let out a whoop of joy and picked her up off her feet and swung her around until she was dizzy. "Marcus put me down you big idiot!" she protested clinging to his muscular shoulders for balance.

"I am sorry baby," he stopped spinning her but held her in his arms. Lydia and Marla had hurried inside the room to find out what the excitement was about. "We are going to be parents," he told them proudly.

"Lord, Marcus, you and your big mouth," Donna said with a groan and punching him on the shoulder. "It's not confirmed yet and my husband was supposed to wait until we are sure before blurting it out."

"We are going to be grandparents?" both women cried out and with a roll of her eyes Donna gave up and let them go ahead with their excitement.

Dinner that Christmas was joyous with the expectancy of a new life and a new addition to their family. Marcus could not contain himself. He kept touching her and looking at her as if he could not believe that she was married to him and was carrying his child inside her.

That night when they went to bed in his bedroom, he lifted her and placed her in the bath filled with warm sudsy water and ran the sponge over her body tenderly. "I don't deserve this," he told her hoarsely, running the sponge over her nipples and lingering there. "I am going to have a family and I don't know what to say. I just want to thank God for you and I love you so much I can't breathe."

The sponge dipped into the water and reached for her mound. Donna gasped as he rubbed the sponge over her and inside her. She gripped his hand and moved against him restlessly. He left the sponge in the water and lifted her out not caring that he was getting all wet as he went with her to the bedroom. "My love," he said softly as he took her lips in a tender kiss that revealed the heart of him.

*****

The doctor confirmed she was four weeks pregnant and as soon as they came out of the doctor's office and got inside the car he broke down in tears. She held him to her as his emotions got the better of him.

He started treating her like Dresden china until Donna got tired of him asking if she was sure she was okay.

"Marcus don't call again unless it's something pertaining to the line we are trying to put out. I love you baby but you are getting on my last nerves." She told him impatiently.

Now that the magazine was such a success they had decide to go ahead with the Wellington Sportswear line. It was already January and they were planning to get it out for Valentine's Day. The ones Donna had modeled were flying off the shelves and had been commissioned by all the large department stores so the demand was great. She had hired an assistant just to appease Marcus and convince him that she was not working too hard.

*****

Her mother called her as soon as they got home that evening. Marcus had a woman come in during the day to take care of what little housework there was but Donna told him that she preferred to do what cooking there was. Besides, they went out to dinner most evenings.

"Hi Mom how are you?" she asked plopping down on the soft leather sofa and blowing her husband a kiss as he pulled off her boots.

"I am okay baby girl. How is my grandchild doing?"

"Your grandchild is doing fine; the mother is not doing so hot. I get nauseous at the drop of a hat and I am gassy all the time." Donna told her, folding her feet underneath her. Marcus had gone straight into the kitchen to prepare some soup for them.

"Welcome to motherhood girl," Lydia said with a laugh. "Do you remember John Franklin?"

"Of course I do!" Donna exclaimed. "Is he okay? I was supposed to go and see him but I have been caught up with everything that's been going on."

"He is not doing so well and he has been asking for you."

"Oh Mom! I have to go and see him. Do you know if they are following up with his visitations?" Donna asked in concern.

"There is a woman who visits him every now and then but I think he misses you honey." Lydia told her.

"I will definitely be by to see him tomorrow." Donna promised. They talked a little bit about church and then her mother told her goodbye.

"Should I be jealous?" Marcus teased as he brought the folding table out for them to have dinner in the living room in front of the fire.

"You should," Donna told him with a smile, making space for him on the sofa and sniffing the stew in appreciation. At least she was not running to the bathroom. He had also placed a loaf of French bread and had prepared a salad as well. "He captured my heart some time ago and I can't seem to stop thinking about him." She told him with an impish smile as he sat beside her and put her bowl in front of her.

"Watch it darling, it doesn't matter that he is all of ninety odd years, I don't tolerate any man longing to see my wife." He growled, reaching down to nip her lip with his teeth.

"I am all yours," she assured him, opening her mouth to capture his tongue. "Always."

They ate and he refused to allow her to wash up the dishes, telling her to relax in front of the television. He came to join her as soon as he was finished and pulled her into his arms while they watched a senseless comedy.

It was sometime later that he realized with amusement that she had fallen asleep in his arms. He picked her up gently, switched off the television and carried her to the bedroom. He removed her clothes trying not to wake her. She did not stir until he was putting her nightgown over her head.

"I fell asleep," she murmured drowsily, giving him a slight smile.

"I didn't notice," he teased her, kissing her on the lips and pulling back the comforter and tucking her in.

"I love you so much," she told him wrapping her hands around his neck.

"I love you too baby."

*****

They went by John Franklin's house on their way to the office. Snow had fallen the night before and the place looked a winter wonderland with the trees all covered up and the pale sun shining on the brilliant whiteness.

They were told to come right in. There was a lady there sitting in a chair by the fire and knitting. "Hi my name is Marge." She told them with a smile. "The agency assigned me to him permanently. He is not doing very well and is confined to his bed now." She told them. She had been expecting them because her mother had called. "She came over with food for him twice per week. Good woman, your mother."

"She sure is," Donna agreed. They went inside the room and Donna was saddened to see how he had deteriorated. He had lost a lot of weight but he recognized her as soon as she came inside the room.

"My dear girl," he stretched out a bony wrinkled hand for her to hold. "And that must be your husband; I hope you realize what a lucky young man you are."

"I do," Marcus said quietly standing inside the doorway and giving them a little space.

"How are you John?" Donna asked in concern. She sat on the side of his bed and held his hands in hers.

"Never better girly," he smiled at her. "Let's talk about you. I hear that big things are happening for you. I saw your beautiful photos in the magazine that your kindly mother brought over for me on one of her visits and I could not put the thing down!" he glanced at Marcus wickedly. "I hope you are not jealous young man but me and this beautiful lady go back a long way."

"I am trying not to be," Marcus said with a small smile.

John laughed and gripped Donna's hands with his. "He's a keeper." He told her softly.

"I know," Donna agreed meeting her husband's eyes. "We are actually having a baby."

"Oh my dear! Congratulations," he said with a wide smile. "I am so happy for you both."

They stayed a little bit even though both of them had meetings to attend. Donna just had a feeling that this was the last time she was going to see him alive.

They left finally, promising that they would try and come and see him again. "My dear girl, you are like a granddaughter to me. You are an incredibly beautiful woman inside and out and I pray that God will bless your little family and watch over you constantly. I want you to know that your visits have meant a lot to me."

"To me too." She told him, kissing him gently on his wrinkled cheek.

"Take care of her," he told Marcus in a serious tone.

"I intend to," he assured the man soberly.

*****

"You okay?" Marcus asked her as they made their way to the office. It was almost eleven o'clock and they had called and canceled the meetings they were supposed to be at.

"I feel a little sad." Donna told him. She pulled the cashmere coat closer to her as she felt a shiver go over her body. Her hair had grown out a little bit and she had combed the front and secured it with pins. "I have a feeling that visit was the last I am going to see of him."

"He does look poorly," Marcus agreed, reaching for her gloved hand and placing it on his thigh, keeping his hand over hers. "He is going to a better place baby and he has lived a full life."

She looked at him gratefully. "Thanks,"

"You're welcome." He told her bringing her hand up to his lips. "Every time."

*****

John died that night and when her mother called her and told her, she cried in her husband's arms. He held her to him until she was spent and afterwards he made love to her. She clung to him as if they were reminding themselves that life was fleeting and they needed to be together whenever they were able to.

The funeral was set for the next weekend and they both went. For a man who had lived so long the turnout was poor including her and Marcus, her mother, his mother and Janet Dawkins from the agency who told her that she was sorely missed. The ceremony was short and after that they went and had dinner at Marla's house before heading back home.

*****

February came and with it the new sports line for both male and female. The magazine carried both of them modeling the gear. It was a big hit and the papers raved over the beautiful couple who made sportswear fashionable and people running to the gym or to find some means of getting healthy.

They were kept busy with orders and planning the next line. Donna refused to slow down. She had not started to show yet although she was three months pregnant and no amount of persuasion from her husband could make her take it easy.

"I have created a monster," Marcus muttered as he threw the ball through the hoop. He was working out his frustration on the court with Tyler. It was almost six o'clock and Donna had asked him to give her another half hour before they headed home.

"She is very good at what she does man, so cut her some slack." Tyler caught the ball that was passed to him. "If she was a man we would not be having this conversation."

"She is not a man and she is pregnant with my child," Marcus said grimly. "It's like she cares more about the damn sportswear than she cares about me or even the child she is carrying."

"I can't believe you just said that." The tone was deceptively quiet and both men turned to stare at the object of their conversation standing at the doorway. Marcus saw the look on her face and his heart sank. What the hell was wrong with him? Tyler put the ball down and made a hasty retreat nodding to Donna briefly.

She looked at him for a few seconds and then turned and walked away. Marcus swore underneath his breath as he hurried after her. "Donna wait!" She did not stop but continued out to the parking lot. He had several cars parked there. She had been using the Porsche and he saw her get inside and close the door. They had never traveled separately before and he could not allow her to do so now but by the time he reached her, she was already backing out.

He jumped into one of the other vehicle not caring that he was still in his shorts and T-shirt he had donned before going onto the court. She was driving too fast, he thought in panic as she raced the car on the slippery road. He picked up the phone to call her to tell her to slow down but he knew she would not answer his calls.

"Please God, please guide her along this slippery road and forgive me for my loose tongue," he prayed desperately as he followed behind her.

To his immense relief she turned onto the road leading to the apartment building and came by just in time to see her hand the keys to Tony who worked at the front before going up. He sat out there in the car for a moment, wondering what he was going to say to her and wondering what sort of damage his comment had made.

He was giddy with the thought of being a father and was probably overdoing it because his father had not been around, but that was no excuse for what he had said about her. She was his wife and even though Tyler was his best friend, he should not have discussed her with him: that was not acceptable. He gripped the steering wheel and looked sightlessly out the window that had frosted up with the cold air and the heat from the car. He got out of the vehicle and as the icy cold hit him he realized he was not dressed for the weather and racing into the building he gave the key to Tony, ignoring the strange look the man gave him as he made his way upstairs to face whatever music there was to face.

*****

Donna took off her winter gear and hung them up carefully. She pulled her nightgown over her head and waited for him to come up. She knew he had been right behind her because she had seen him in the rear view mirror of the car. She knew she had been driving too fast and she knew better but she had been hurt and angry at what he had said and that he had said it to Tyler instead of her.

She ran her hands over the slight bump of her belly and sat down on the bed wondering if he was right. Was she so busy caught up in what she was doing that she was not thinking about him or their baby? She had decided she was never going back to that world again but was she being snared back inside it? She had asked God to keep her focused on him and on her marriage and whatever came after. She had gotten so excited about the magazine, the gear and the designing of it. Besides, she was taking her vitamins and making sure she got enough sleep at night, what more was she supposed to do? And where was he?

She was in the kitchen drinking a cup of tea to settle her stomach when she heard the door open. Her back was turned towards the door and she felt his presence rather than saw him standing in the doorway. "Can we talk?"

"Now you want to talk?" she did not turn around but continued to sip her tea. He came around to face her and Donna realized that he was shivering a little bit, probably due to his mad rush from the gym and trying to catch up with her.

"Donna please," he looked chastened and defeated. "I spoke out of terms. I was frustrated about you working so hard and I voiced something that should have been said only to you. Baby, can you at least look at me?" he pleaded.

She did and her heart hitched as she saw the penitent expression on his face. "I am looking," she told him coolly, still not ready to let him off the hook.

"I grew up without a father as you know and the thought of being a father scares me and excites me at the same time. I want to be the best father a child could ever have and I am afraid I will not make a good father. I-"

"Stop!" she leaned forward and put a finger against his lips. "You are an incredible man and husband and have been a good son to your mother. You are not your father Marcus and for you to even think that!" She gave an impatient shrug. "I am new to this too and I have hang ups and questions and fears but I know that I can put everything in God's hands and he will direct us the right way. I know I have been caught up with this business at work but I love what I do. It does not mean that I will neglect you or our baby. It's God then you and no amount of excitement at work or anything else will change that. God, you are such an idiot!" she finished in exasperation.

"Yes I am," he admitted sheepishly, glad that he was no longer in the dog house. "I am sorry baby."

"Okay apology accepted." She told him coming around to him. "You are cold and wet," she ran her hands over his muscled arms trying to warm him up. "I am going to run you a warm bath while you drink some of that tea."

"I love you very much you know that?" he rested his forehead against hers.

"You had better," she warned and kissing him softly on the lips, she went to the bathroom.

*****

Later that night as they lay in bed after she had pulled up a stool and run the sponge over his body; and after many interruptions during which he had insisted she joined him in the tub; he held her in his arms as she rested her head on his shoulder.

"I am going to work shorter hours." She murmured softly.

"Baby, I overreacted and I am sorry." He tightened his hold on her. "You are very good at what you do, you were born for it. You have increased sales a hundred percent and the magazine cannot stay on the shelves because of you. You did it and I am so proud of you baby and I am sorry for being so pigheaded and totally male. I want you to continue and if you feel tired or stressed then you slow down."

"I promise," she lifted her head to look at him, his chocolate brown face and the slight overgrowth of hair on his strong jaw. "You are going to make a great father and I am positive about that."

"Thanks baby," he brought his head up to hers and kissed her softly.

"What are we going to name it?" She asked a little later on after a few moments of silence.

"How about Benjamin if it's a boy and Brianna if it's a girl." He suggested with a grin.

"Absolutely not!" Donna lifted her head to look at him, punching him lightly on the chest. "I see I am going to have to come up with the names and not leave it to you. How about Daniel if it's a boy and Lydia Marla if it's a girl."

He clasped her face between his hands and looked at her tenderly. "I think it's a great idea!"

Chapter 9

August rolled in with temperatures reaching in the high nineties and the humidity bringing it up further. She was scheduled to have baby by the eighth of August and she could not wait. She had stopped going to the office but spent time at home organizing the nursery.

Margaret, the day helper was a blessing and helped her put up the pale blue and yellow wall paper because she had insisted on doing it herself even though Marcus had said he would hire someone to do it. They were having a boy and her husband was over the moon and could not wait until Daniel Marcus Wellington made his appearance. He had put up some of his basketball pictures all over the nursery and there was a ball holding prominence on the strong oak dresser he had bought to put his son's clothes in.

"I am telling you Mom, it's like he is obsessed," Donna grumbled good-naturedly as they placed the mobile over the crib. Lydia had come over that morning to lend a helping hand. Donna had stopped going out since she was so near to giving birth; so her mother and Marla had taken to coming around two times for the week. They usually came together but Marla had a doctor's appointment so Lydia had come by herself.

"He is not the only one," Lydia told her with a smile as she folded the clothes she had brought and put them away in one of the drawers.

"You are right," Donna said shaking her head as she sat down on one of the several comfortable rockers in the room. "You, Marla and my husband are bent on buying out every single baby clothes that has ever been made and not to mention toys. I had to threaten Marcus that if he ever came back with another suit of clothes or stuffed toy that I am going to take all of them off the shelves and give them away."

"Can you blame him?" Lydia defended her son in law. "The man is in high heavens. He is having a family and he is excited about it. There are so many men who are of our color who do not give two cents about the child or children they bring into this world. It's admirable and refreshing to see someone who does."

"I know mom and I thank God for that every day," Donna acknowledged leaning back against the cushion of the chair and closing her eyes briefly taking deep breaths. Sometimes the baby seemed to be lodge somewhere near her lungs and it was hard for her to breathe. "Just the other day I was talking to a sister who told me that the man she had been with had gone and left her with two children to take care of. I want to reach out to help those who are in that position. I have asked Marcus to let us set up a foundation for children whose fathers are missing in action. Not only to hand out clothes, toys or money but to be a sort of surrogate father where those children can have someone to talk to and have a positive male influence in their lives."

"That's a wonderful idea honey!" her mother said in approval. "Sometimes we sit in our tidy little world and forget that there are people out there who are going through immense suffering and would like to find someone to lend a helping hand. Count me in darling and whatever I can do to help, I will."

"We are actually using the sales from the magazine and we are soliciting help from other organizations as well. There is this young man who comes around to play basketball with Marcus and those at work and he has such potential. He wants to be a doctor," Donna said with a smile. "But he has no father figure in his life and his mother is working minimum wage so we are seeking funding to send him to college. We are also looking at the possibility of him getting a full scholarship."

"My dear I am so proud of you! Praise the Lord!" Lydia had tears in her eyes as she came over and hugged her daughter. "We are here to help each other and that's the way God intended it to be!"

*****

"How about a massage?" Marcus came and sat on the edge of the bed.

He had come home late because of a meeting. He had called her and told her he was running late and that she was not to go into labor before he reached her. "I will try my best," she had told him dryly.

Now he was home and she had been waiting up for him, reading an inspirational novel. She had been feeling a little uncomfortable and even after her mother had left and Margaret had left for the evening she had been having difficulty breathing so she had decided to retire early.

"Sounds like a lovely idea." She eased up onto the mound of pillows and turned on her side. He was still in his work clothes, he had taken off his sports jacket, hung it on the peg in the room and took off his shirt, leaving only the white T-shirt.

"I see you and your mother had fun in the nursery," he teased as he went behind her and started massaging the small of her back. Donna sighed in contentment as he rubbed her back.

"And I bet I see another stuffed toy in there that you bought," she said with a sigh.

"You will certainly not see another stuffed toy, I just happened to be passing by a toy store and I saw the cutest little rattler and I just had to buy it." He told her with a grin. "So you see, I have not been disobedient one bit."

"Darling you have to stop buying stuff for the baby. I understand how excited you are but don't you think he has enough things?"

He turned her gently around to face him, smoothing the wisps of curls from her cheeks as he looked at her tenderly. He could not help but feel something well up inside him as soon as he saw her swollen with his child inside her. How had he gotten to be so blessed?

"I know when to stop and I know that there are kids around who have nothing to look forward to but this is my son. I promise you that I will never ignore the needs of others around me but please let me spoil him and you a little." His fingers traced her lips and she felt the desire rise inside her.

"A little?" she asked him in amusement.

"Okay a hell of a lot." He admitted, bending his head to capture her lips with his. "A whole lot." His hand reached between her legs and parted them, easing away her underwear and touching her; his fingers searching and finding her core and working his way deep inside her. "Let me spoil you some more," he whispered huskily and set about doing so.

*****

August the eight dawned bright with expectancy. It was the time the doctor had given for her to give birth and Donna had to admit that she could not wait to put down the load she was carrying. Her belly was making her steps slow and laborious and she was finding it difficult to finish the slightest task. She had been relying on Marcus and the helper, Margaret and she found that she was sleeping a lot even during the days.

"I am not going in today," Marcus announced as they were eating breakfast together that morning.

"Why not?" she looked up at him curiously. Usually by now he would be half dressed but she noticed that he was still in his bathrobe and he had not gone to take a shower. He had brought her breakfast in bed because even though she had not told him, he knew she had not had a very good night so he had had Margaret prepared the breakfast and taken it to her.

"Today happens to be your due date, have you forgotten?" He took the tray away from her and placed it on the bedside table.

"No but you are just a telephone call away and besides you have that very important meeting that you yourself set up for today." Donna reminded him as she rested back against the pillows. He had helped her take a shower and had made sure to pack her bags, ready to leave at the slightest notice.

"I am not going," he said stubbornly. "I will call and reschedule."

"Honey these people are coming all the way from out of town for a meeting you called remember?" she reminded him patiently. "We are trying to get the funding in place for the community center and to get them interested in putting up some money to form a scholarship fund for the children who want to go to college and university but are not able to afford it, you cannot stay away."

He sighed heavily as what she had just said dawned on him. "I can't leave you Donna, what if something happens?"

"To make you feel better I'll call our moms and Margaret is here. I promise you that even if I am in excruciating pain I will call you." Donna reassured him.

"Okay," he said grudgingly getting up to go and get dressed. "I will be calling you every few minutes." He warned her. "And baby; if you feel the slightest twinge please call me."

"I promise."

*****

"Marcus I have to tell you, this is a very worthwhile venture and I am glad you have suggested it." David Brenna, the chief executive of a software company said with a pleased smile. He was a balding man in his late fifties and had dark skin that looked like burnt chocolate. He had a merry laugh and a paunch that spoke of soft living.

"I am glad to be a part of it a well," another African American said. He owned a fleet of restaurants and had grown up without a father figure in his life. "I am trying to get more people on board so that we can run with this as soon as possible." There was a chorus of agreement around the large round table. They were in his conference room, it was approaching five o'clock and the meeting was still in full swing.

"I understand your wife was the one who came up with this idea Marcus. How is she doing by the way, I read somewhere that she was pregnant?" Michael Moore asked. He was a famous African American actor and had come on board when Marcus had asked him to.

"She is actually due today so I have been checking up on her ever so often." Marcus told them. He had called her a short while ago and she had told him that she was okay and not in labor yet; the same answer she had given a few minutes ago when he had called.

"Marcus can you do me a favor, don't call me again for the rest of the evening? You will be home shortly and I want to get a little nap." She had told him.

"So what are you doing here man?" Michael asked him in surprise, raising bushy brows sprinkled with gray.

"My wife reminded me I had this meeting to attend and I was the one who had called it." Marcus said with a grim smile.

"Then this meeting is over," Michael told him firmly. "We are all on board and you will be hearing from us soon. Go be with your wife." The others sitting around the table agreed and the meeting broke up.

*****

The pain started the next day at four a.m. She had felt slight twinges while she had been having dinner with Marcus after he came home. He had kept calling her every few minutes as he had promised. Donna felt impatient but reminded herself that he was as scared as she was. Her mother and Marla had spent almost the entire day with her and had been at her beck and call for the day along with Margaret. They had left only when they knew Marcus was on his way home.

The sharp pain woke her up and she gasped, unconsciously gripping Marcus' hand around her extended belly. "Honey?" he said sleepily, raising his head slightly.

Donna took a deep breath. "I just felt something I don't know if it's time."

He reached over and switched on the bedside lamp. Her face was tensed and her hands were clenched. As soon as he reached for the phone to call Dr. Peters she let out a little gasp, her hand going to her belly. "It is time," he said grimly.

"Dr. Peters, I think my wife is in labor," he said as soon as the doctor answered. He listened for a moment then looked at her. Her face had relaxed but her hands were still gripping the sheets. "He wants to know how far apart the contractions are." Just then another wave of pain hit her with full force and she cried out in agony. "I am bringing her in." he told the doctor briefly, and without waiting for his response he hung up the phone.

"My water just broke," she gasped and Marcus saw the bloody mucus on the sheets between her legs. He went inside the bathroom quickly, his heart hammering and his legs barely carrying him but he forced himself to be calm. He tidied her up and changed her clothes including her underwear. While he was going downstairs he called their mothers.

He reached the car, buckled her in and drove off, all the time telling her to breathe. The traffic was light on the road at that hour and he made his way towards the hospital quickly, placing one hand on her thigh as she rode out another painful contraction.

"We are almost there baby; just hang on," he said desperately trying to keep his panic from showing.

"I am okay Marcus," she told him leaning back against the headrest wearily. "It will be worth it soon."

The doctor briskly instructed the nurse to help her into the wheelchair and they wheeled her straight into the labor ward.

"Do you want to stay with her?" Dr. Peters asked Marcus as he got ready to attend to her.

"Try and keep me out," he said grimly as Donna gripped his hand.

The labor was long and even though they had given her something to help with the pain, the baby was taking longer than expected. Both Lydia and Marla were in the waiting room and Marcus had been out there briefly to let them know the progress.

The sun had come up and it was almost nine o'clock in the morning. "You're doing very well baby," Marcus assured her as he wiped the perspiration from her face. Her hand trembled slightly and Marcus knew she was exhausted. He had seen the doctor in consulting with the nurses and had demanded to know if something was wrong.

"It's just that the baby is not coming fast enough and your wife's strength is waning. We were thinking of doing a c-section if she has not given birth in the next hour." Dr. Peters told him frankly.

Use a knife on her? Marcus was horrified. With a sudden decision he told the doctor and nurses. "Can you leave us alone for a moment?"

The doctor started to disagree and seeing the expression on his face he nodded. "We will give you a minute."

"Listen baby." He said wiping her face, she had her eyes closed but she opened them and smiled at him. "Our son is being very stubborn and has refused to come out of your very warm and comfortable womb. My mom and yours are in the waiting room praying and I think we should do our part as well. What do you think?"

"You want us to pray?" she whispered.

"I want us to pray." He nodded.

"I am in agreement." She told him softly and closed her eyes.

"Heavenly Father, here we are before you to humbly ask for your help in bringing our son into this world. The doctor has so much power but you have the ultimate power. We are asking you to use that power to bring our child into the world. My wife is exhausted and I am asking you to give her the strength. I hate to see her like this Lord and I am asking you to give her your strength in Jesus' name. Amen."

"That was lovely," she told him with a smile, giving his hand a squeeze.

"Thanks baby." He said just as the doctor and nurses came back in. "Ready to do this?" he asked her.

"Ready," she told him with a nod.

"All right Mrs. Wellington do not push until I tell you to." Dr. Peters instructed her.

Their son was born fifteen minutes later and Marcus was not afraid to tell everyone that it was the power of prayer that dislodged his son from his wife's womb.

Marcus held his son in his arms the minute they cleaned him up. Donna had barely looked at him before she drifted off to sleep because of sheer exhaustion. Both their mothers had seen him and exclaimed what a beautiful baby he was. He weighed in at seven pounds eight ounces and he had his mother's complexion and eyes and looked very much like his father.

"Welcome to the club bro," Tyler who had come over with flowers and cards from work said slapping him on the back. They were looking in the nursery where his son was sleeping after he had been fed by one of the nurses. "How does it feel to be a father?"

"Humbling," Marcus said with a catch in his throat. He had felt the tears starting when his son had come out crying loudly, proving there was nothing wrong with his lungs. He had hugged his wife to him and rested his forehead against hers and told her thanks. "And scared. I am going to be responsible for someone else's life and I am afraid I am going to make a lot of mistakes."

"There is one guide book that works very well," Tyler told him. Marcus looked at him enquiringly.

"The Bible bro," Tyler said. "The greatest guide book in the world."

Donna woke up two hours later starving. Marcus ordered burgers and fries for her because that was what she felt like eating. Lydia and Marla had gone home to come back later but he had not left. He had taken a quick shower in her bathroom and pulled on a T-shirt and shorts Tyler had picked up for him. He was not leaving without her.

"He is perfect." She said softly as she looked down at their son. She had just breastfed him and burped him and he was looking up at them in contentment. "Daniel Marcus Wellington welcome to the family. You are going to be so loved and spoiled that I am going to have to tell your father no more." She looked up at her husband who was lying beside her looking at both of them.

"You better believe it," he said with a grin, using one of his fingers to touch his son's bunched up fist. "He has your eyes," he added. He was on top of the world and he could not believe that he was right here with his family. What a privilege.

"And your everything else," Donna told him softly. "I love you Marcus and Daniel, the two men in my life. Thank God."

*****

She was released two days after and he was there along with their mothers to travel with her and her son from the hospital. Lydia had baked and Margaret had cooked in anticipation of their coming and there was a welcome home banner in the living room that said 'welcome home Donna and Daniel'. Marcus took their son from her as soon as they went inside the nursery and made sure she was comfortable in one of the rockers.

"It's so good to be home," Donna said with a sigh. "Hospitals are not my favorite places."

"He is so perfect," Marla was looking at her grandson with tears in her eyes. "He looks like you when you were born Marcus." She told her son.

"He's going to be a heartbreaker one of these days." Lydia said as she stood beside Marla and looked at him.

"He already is," Donna said softly, holding her husband's hand as he came to join her on the rocker. She rested her head on his shoulder, contented and happy to be with her family.

Chapter 10

A month and a half later

"I think he gets bigger each time I see him." Lydia commented as she lifted her grandson into her arms.

They were at the house and Donna had just finished breastfeeding her son. The time she had spent at home with him had made her realize how precious he was and how much she loved being a mother. He was a very good baby only waking him one time during the night to be fed or changed.

"I am going back to the office in another two weeks." Donna commented touching her son's soft cheek gently. They were in the nursery in the afternoon. It was Thursday and October and already the time had become chilly. She had spoken to Marcus about going back and he had told her that the decision was entirely up to her.

"You are going to hire someone?" Lydia asked her.

"I hate to think of a stranger taking care of my child." Donna said with a helpless shrug. "I have been praying about it."

"I have a suggestion." Lydia placed the sleepy baby back inside the crib, rubbing his tummy affectionately. "Marla and I have been talking and we want to spend time with our grandson and we do not want some stranger taking care of him either. So how about; both of us take care of him while you go back out?"

Donna stared at her in surprise, the idea appealing to her a lot. "Mom are you sure?"

"I can do my baking from here in your lovely kitchen and while I am out delivering, both Marla and Margaret are here to look over Daniel." Lydia told her with a smile.

"Oh Mom!" Donna said in a hushed voice going over to hug her. "I think that's an answer to my prayers and it's a great plan."

"Okay honey then it's settled. You will have to discuss it with your husband of course."

"I know he's going to say a resounding yes!"

*****

He did say yes. That night as they stood there looking down at their son sleeping with his bottom in the air. Donna had been working on another line of gym wear for children. The scholarship funding had been going very well with two children already gone off to colleges. She had also turned the basketball court into not only somewhere balls go into the hoops but also a place where the surrogate fathers got to interact with the kids who came there.

Marcus had looked on proudly at what she had turned the company into. His wife was a genius when it came to business with a heart.

"I knew you did not want someone coming in here and taking care of our son so I think it's a perfect solution." Marcus commented. "The only thing is we are going to pay them as normal employees."

"I don't think they will agree to that but I will let them know." She snuggled up against him and rested her head against his shoulder. She breathed in his special scent of something woodsy and expensive. "I can't help thinking how blessed we are and we have so much to give God thanks for. I wonder if we are doing enough to show God how much we appreciate all of these blessings."

He led them away from Daniel's crib and out of the room, making sure that the monitor and night light was on before going into their bedroom.

He had changed and showered already and he sat with her on the lounge chair. "I have never met a woman like you with such a big heart." He told her in a soft voice. "You have turned a company that I built into something special and wonderful. You are reaching out to children and parents alike and giving them hope and I think that's a lot. You are the most generous person I know and it amazes me that a woman as beautiful as you could care so much about people. I have got to be the most blessed brother in the entire world!"

Donna felt tears coming to her eyes at her husband's words and she thanked God that he had opened up her heart to accept his love. "I love you Marcus Wellington." She whispered and sank into his arms. He held her against him and thanked God for sending her to him at that precise moment when he did.

*****

"I want cheerful colors," Donna looked at the fabric with a little frown. It was her first day back at work. She had fed and kissed her son and left him in the capable arms of Marla and Lydia who looked forward to taking care of their grandson. "I don't want you to be calling every few minutes to find out how your son is doing. He is in capable hands." Marla told them firmly.

"We will try not to," Donna said with a smile as she went from the room.

Marcus had hired an assistant; a totally eccentric woman by the name of 'Birdie'. "What is her real name? Surely her parents could not have named her Birdie?" Donna asked in amusement. She had to admit that the name suited her as she was always flitting from here to there. She had raven black hair that was cut in an absurd style that stuck up on top of her head but her beautiful green eyes were always twinkling. She had done art in college and she was very good at designing things.

"My real name is Betty-Ann Clarke," she said coming inside the room, she had on a pair of orange pants and a purple blouse with green frills. "I prefer the name Birdie."

"Then Birdie it is." Donna told her solemnly.

They worked well together and things she did not see Donna picked up on. Like a flaw in the fabric or the wrong color and shade and she had a pretty good idea what people wanted.

"I always admire your photos in the magazines," the woman commented one day when they were in Donna's office playing around with a design. "You were far from looking like those totally unreal models that they wanted us to believe were real. When I saw you in person I was bowled over by how much you look the same or even better." She said with an impish grin.

"Thanks, I think," Donna said smiling at the girl. It was almost four o'clock and she realized she had not called home in the past two hours being so caught up with work.

"What a beautiful child!" Birdie picked up the framed photo of Daniel that she had taken with her to the office. Marcus had a picture of her and their son while they were in the hospital and one taken at home where she was holding their son and smiling for the camera. She also had a photo of her and Marcus when they were getting married on her desk.

"He sure is," Donna said softly. "I haven't called to find out how he is doing for the last two hours. My mother and mother in law must be so relieved."

"They are the ones taking care of little cutie?" Birdie put the framed photo back on the desk.

"Yes," Donna said absently her mind already on the design Birdie had come up with. "What about this color?" she asked holding up a material in emerald green.

"Perfect!" Birdie exclaimed. "Now if we add a slash of purple in the middle then it's a go!"

*****

She and Marcus went home together at six and they talked about the day. "How was your first day back at work?" he asked her as he drove out of the parking garage.

"Interesting," she told him, a glimmer in her dark brown eyes. "We are making progress with the new line and I really like Birdie, she knows her stuff and she is very interesting."

"I am glad." He glanced at her briefly. She was wearing a chic maroon blouse and black pants and had thrown a multicolored shawl around the blouse that looked startling against her coffee and cream skin. She was wearing ruby knobs that glinted at her lobes and matching bracelets. She looked cool and incredibly beautiful and he could not get over the fact that she was his wife and the mother of his son. She had reshaped her hair and it lay flat on her scalp; the style uniquely hers.

"How about us going somewhere this weekend?" he asked her lightly. They had not been together physically since she had given birth and he found himself aching for her every single minute.

"I am way ahead of you there mister," she told him flashing a smile. "I have asked Mom and Marla to house swap. So they will be coming to stay with us this weekend and we are going to be spending the weekend at Marla's"

They had arrived at the apartment and he switched off the car and turned to look at her. "You're incredible, do you know that?" he said shaking his head.

"I know," she whispered moving closer to him to take his lips with hers. "I miss feeling you inside me."

*****

Marla and Lydia were not half ready to go home as they claimed they were having fun with their grandson. Daniel was still up and making little cooing sounds as his grandmothers stood court around him.

"How was your first day back honey?" Lydia asked as she placed the bathed and fed Daniel into her daughter's arms.

"Profitable," Donna nuzzled her baby to her inhaling his scent of powder and baby oil. "Thanks you guys for taking care of him. I did not feel the need to call so much."

"It's out pleasure," Marla answered with a smile. "This little man is so quiet that we hardly believed a baby was in the house."

*****

That night she woke up to find that Marcus was not on the bed beside her. With a resigned smile she went quietly in the direction of the nursery and heard his voice. She stopped and listened as he spoke to his son.

"I am still in awe that I am your father buddy," he said softly as his son cooed away. "I am still trying to recover from the fact that your mother married me. Both of you mean so much to me that I find myself thanking God every chance I get for the wonderful blessings of having you guys in my life. I would give up my entire company if I had to choose and there is nothing that will ever come before you guys. Your mom is such a terrific lady and I find myself worrying that I am going to disappoint her in some way. I am proud of her and the way she handles herself, we are so blessed to have her in our lives and we are going to be showing her that every day."

Donna crept back into the bedroom knowing that what he had just said was something private. She knelt beside the bed and prayed. "My Father in Heaven, I want to thank you for giving me a family such as the one I have. I don't deserve anything good from you but because of your grace and mercy, you have blessed me so much. I do not ever want to take your blessings for granted and I am asking you to help me to be the best wife and mother to my husband and son. I am asking for directions and for you to remind me that I am asking you for these. I cannot do this by myself and I am asking for your help in all these things in Jesus' name. Amen."

She heard when he came back into the room and got on the bed beside her. Even when he put his arm around her she pretended to be asleep and smiled when he whispered: "I love you."

*****

Donna packed for them for the weekend. They were going to go straight from the office to Marla's house and both her mother and Marla had arrived armed with weekend bags and enough baking products to fill a bakery.

"I have orders for several places this weekend." Lydia said with a smile.

Marla had already taken charge of Daniel and was bouncing her grandson on her lap. "Watch it mom, he just ate." Marcus told her.

"Oops sorry honey," she put the baby onto her shoulder and rubbed his back gently.

"So we will see you on Monday evening," Donna said looking down at her son, very torn to be leaving him for three whole nights, but it was worth it and she need to spend some time with her husband as well, they needed that.

"He will be okay," Marcus told her as he came behind her and pulled her into his arms.

"I know." She kissed him softly on the cheek and Marcus took him in his arms and held for a little bit. "See you soon buddy," he said kissing him on the forehead.

*****

They left work at six and headed out. "You okay?" he asked her. She had been quiet since they got in the vehicle.

"Just feel strange not going home to see our son." She admitted.

"Want to change your mind?" he asked her, holding his breath for her reply.

"Of course not!" Donna told him. "I am really looking forward to us being alone together."

She changed out of her work clothes and cooked for him, refusing to accept his offer of help in the kitchen.

"Something smells delicious, what's on the menu?" Marcus asked coming into the large homey kitchen and sniffing the air.

"Chicken Fettuccine and pumpkin rice and I made a salad."
She told him. She was wearing tiny shorts that rode up high
on her buttocks and a tight T-shirt and no bra. Even though
she had put on one of Marla's apron, every time she bent over
to look in the oven at the fruit cake she had in there, he was
given an enticing view of her pubic and he could see that she
was not wearing any underwear. He did not know if he could
wait until after dinner to have her, he was as hard as a rock.

"How about we skip dinner?" he had come up behind her as
she stood around the stove, tasting the rice.

"I thought you were starving?" she queried, turning off the
stove and turning to face him. he moved her away from the
stove and took off her apron, his eyes zeroing in on her
unfettered breasts still laden with his son's milk, the nipples
pressing against the material.

"I am," he murmured, pulling the shirt over her head. "But not
for food." He bent his head and captured a nipple inside his
mouth.

Donna gasped as his mouth closed over her pebble like nipple
and she had to hold onto him to keep her balance as he pulled
on it urgently, his hands pulling down the tiny terry shorts. She

stepped out of them and stood completely naked before him. He released her breast and stepped back, looking at her exquisite body that only a couple of months ago had carried his child inside it. She now looked like she had never given birth. Her stomach had gone back to its original flatness and there was not an ounce of stretch marks on her beautiful skin. Apart from her breasts being fuller, she looked the same. "Beautiful," he said thickly and lifting her up into his arms he carried her towards the bedroom that was his when he visited his mother.

He placed her on the bed and pulled his shirt over his head, next came his shorts and underwear. He stood there looking at her, his penis stiff and ready for her. "I want to eat you," he told her hoarsely.

"I want that too," Donna said huskily, opening her legs wide.

With a growl he pulled her to the edge of the bed and placed his mouth on her, lifting her legs over his head as his tongue delved inside her opening liking and savoring her scent.

Donna gripped the sheets tightly as the sensation of pleasure invaded her body and she bucked against his mouth, a cry escaping her lips.

He stood up and without a word he entered her wrapping her legs around his waist. Her tightness wrap around his erection pulling him in and he had to grit his teeth to keep from crying out. He thrust inside her and when she returned the thrusts he increased the pace, his breathing turning shallow as he moved against her, his control slipping. This was what he had been patiently waiting for ever since she had given birth. The pleasure of being inside her, a part of her, reaching deep inside her as she wrapped herself around him. No other woman has ever made him feel like he was crashing into something incredible except her, his wife.

He felt his testicles tightening and knew he would not last long. He knew they had the whole weekend but he wanted to prolong the moment, this moment. He pulled out of her and Donna cried out at the loss of him inside her and watched as he held his penis wet with her juice between his closed fist and stared at her, his dark eyes half closed as he looked at her.

He climbed over her and put his penis between her breasts and moved towards her lips. She took him inside her mouth and as her mouth closed over him he sagged over her, his body bucking as he moved inside her mouth. He pulled out when he felt himself coming and quickly changed position and entered her forcefully, pulling her legs up and thrusting inside her urgently over and over again.

They came together; the combined orgasm hitting them with such force that they cried out from it. He lifted her against him and captured her mouth with his in a desperation that transferred itself to her. She clung to him tightly, clinging to him and her lips moving over his hungrily as she moved her body against his, her body shivering from the aftermath of her orgasm.

He climbed on the bed with her, their lips still clinging to each other, their bodies still bound together as they waited for the shivering to come to a stop.

"I love you," he told her passionately, his hands framing her exquisite face. He was still semi erect inside her and he had no intention of coming out right away, he could not. "I love you so much that I cannot explain it in words; I can only try to say it with my body. Donna I don't know how and why you are in my life. Sometimes I have to pinch myself to find out if I am really dreaming but I promise I will never hurt you intentionally, I can't because I love you too much."

"I love you too and I thank God for you, for my son. I have a family and I thank Him for allowing that to happen. I won't hurt you either because hurting you means hurting myself. I love you my husband, my partner, my best friend and aside from my love of God my savior, it is you."

He moved inside her slowly and his lips met hers in a soft kiss that had her holding to him tightly. For the next half hour they explored each other until they were exhausted and sated.

"How about having some of that delicious dinner you prepared?" he asked her lazily, kissing her brow and coming down to her cheeks.

"I think that's a very good idea." She told him teasingly. She moved away, getting ready to put on a robe.

"Uh uh," he said. "No clothes. I want to look at every inch of your body while you are dishing out the food and I want to be able to take a nipple inside my mouth while I am eating, not to mention putting my finger inside you when the need arises," he grinned at her wickedly as he climbed off the bed to join her.

"You're insatiable." She said shaking her head and putting away the robe.

"Only when it comes to you." He whispered softly as he pulled her up against him. They did not make it to dinner for the next hour.

The end.

If you enjoyed this ebook and want me to keep writing more, please leave a review of it on the store where you bought it. By doing so you'll allow me more time to write these books for you as they'll get more exposure. So thank you. :)

Get Free Romance eBooks!

Hi there. As a special thank you for buying this book, for a limited time I want to send you some great ebooks completely **free of charge** directly to your email! You can get it by going to this page:

www.saucyromancebooks.com/physical

You can see a the cover of these books on the next page:

These ebooks are so exclusive you can't even buy them. When you download them I'll also send you updates when new books like this are available.

Again, that link is:

www.saucyromancebooks.com/physical

Now, if you enjoyed the book you just read, please leave a positive review of it where you bought it (e.g. Amazon). It'll help get it out there a lot more and mean I can continue writing these books for you. So thank you. :)

More Books By Shannon Gardener

If you enjoyed that, you'll love Saving Grace by Shannon Gardener (sample and description of what it's about below -

search 'Saving Grace by Shannon Gardener' on Amazon to get it now).

Description:

Grace has been through a lot.

She grew up in the ghetto, her dad has been shot after making his money illegally, and she's now homeless.

Thankfully though, her aunt and uncle have taken her in and are ready to provide a better influence.

Being convinced by her aunt she may be able to find peace at church, Grace soon attends a local service.

She would've been happy with finding inner peace and discovering God, but Grace soon finds more than she imagined at church.

Namely the deacon Peter, an attractive and rich man with a good heart.

But with the two with such different backgrounds and views of life, can they find a common ground for a true love to start?

Want to read more? Then search 'Saving Grace Shannon Gardener' on Amazon to get it now.

Also available: A Match Made in Heaven by Ashlie Brooks (search 'A Match Made in Heaven Ashlie Brooks' on Amazon to get it now).

Description:

Janelle Peters didn't know what to expect from her first produced game show, but it certainly wasn't to end up starring in it!

Right before the first episode of Match Made In Heaven goes to air, one of the female contestants backs out and Janelle has no choice but to step in.

Handsome bachelor Reece James is instructed to vote her off in the first round, but when they get to talking on the show she finds out they have more in common than she ever thought possible.

Soon Reece and Janelle start to spend a lot of off-camera time together, and they quickly realize that they're falling head over heels in love.

However, there's one thing that Janelle doesn't know about Reece, and he isn't sure how to break the news...

Are the two a match made in heaven?

Want to read more? Then search 'A Match Made in Heaven Ashlie Brooks' on Amazon to get it now.

You can also see other related books by myself and other top romance authors at:

www.saucyromancebooks.com/romancebooks